T0619474

Between the Words

Between the Words

HOLLY JACOBS

Copyright The characters and events in these stories are fictitious.
Any similarities to real people, living or dead, is coincidence and not
intended by the author.

Ilex Books 2018
ISBN-13: 978-1-948311-00-7

Copyright Holly Fuhrmann
All Rights Reserved

Cover by Kim Van Meter

To Brenda and Craig Smith and everyone at Smith Farms.
Thanks for the tour ... and all the eggs!

Table of Contents

I NEVER HAD big dreams.

No, my dreams were built of small things.

Maybe they were dreams of another era.

I dreamed of a man who would love me.

A man I could love.

I dreamed of a house filled with children.

I dreamed of a perfect life.

And I thought I'd found that perfect life of my dreams.

I married a man I loved and I thought he loved me, too. We had a son and then a daughter. We lived in a big house in a lovely neighborhood.

I reveled in that small, ordinary life.

And then on a winter Monday, in the midst of a snowstorm, someone knocked on my front door and my small, perfect life shattered.

I couldn't have known then that perfection is overrated.

I didn't understand that the biggest things in life are made up of the smallest ones. They're built of small moments that grow from other small moments until one day you look back and realize that your life isn't small in the least.

And it's certainly not perfect.

Life is imperfect. It's messy.

And that imperfection is the stuff that our dreams are made of.

If you listen between the words, watch between the moments, you'll see that life is perfectly imperfect.

And it turns out, so is love.

But I hadn't learned that on that snowy Monday as I opened my front door ...

Prologue

Alice

*On the plus side: Strangers can turn out to
be friends we haven't met yet.*

"Haley and Jeremy," I yelled for the umpteenth time as I checked the pantry with its shelves lined with glass storage containers. Each container had a chalkboard label on it. All those labeled jars were arranged oh-so orderly in my pantry.

It was a little thing that made me happy. And frankly, today with two kids home for a snow-day, I was grasping at any little happy straw.

I know that many people don't enjoy a Friday the thirteenth, but I decided that Monday the thirteenth was no picnic either.

Especially in January with winter winds beating at the door and lake effect storm warnings interrupting television shows and sending alerts to my cellphone.

There was another loud thump coming from upstairs, followed by a high-pitched squeal.

"If I have to come up there ..." I left the threat open-ended as I shut the pantry door.

Jeremy and Haley were gifted with wonderful imaginations and I knew that I could never come up with a threat half as terrifying as they could make up on their own.

The thumping stopped immediately.

I smiled to myself as I walked into the living room and lit a fire in the fireplace.

Yes, those lake effect warnings were right. Thick, heavy flakes pelted against my windows as the cold Canadian wind blew across Lake Erie, picking up all that lake moisture and dumping it down as snow on Erie, Pennsylvania—the city that sat on the lake's southern shore.

My doorbell rang and almost immediately someone started thumping on the door itself.

Who on earth would venture out in weather like this? Maybe it was Alan? In which case why wouldn't he use his key?

The questions tumbled over themselves as I hurried to the door. I opened it and found myself staring at a stranger. I couldn't place the strange woman who frowned at me.

She was a very pregnant woman. She was bundled in a black pea coat that didn't look warm enough to begin with and was even less protection against the cold because it no longer buttoned over her huge stomach.

Inviting strangers into the house wasn't my standard operating procedure but given the storm that was raging outside I couldn't *not* invite her in. And frankly her pregnancy was so obvious that I felt confident she couldn't be much of a threat to me even if she'd wanted to be.

"Come in," I said and ushered her into the foyer.

I shut the door behind her. "It's awful out there. I can't believe you were out driving in this storm."

The woman didn't say anything as she took off her gloves and her black woolen hat, which let her long blonde hair spill out. It stood starkly against her jacket as she studied me and shot me a look that had me rethinking inviting her in.

"I'm sorry. How can I help you?" I asked.

"Are you Alice Collins?" she asked. I could hear the anger that was just below the surface of her innocuous inquiry. Between those words anger reverberated, becoming as audible as the words themselves. She stuffed her hat and gloves in her coat pocket with far more force than necessary.

"Yes," I answered slowly.

I had no idea what I could have done to make this stranger—and I was sure she was a stranger—so mad. "And you are?"

"I don't know what I thought," she mused more to herself than said to me. "It seems like it would be easier to navigate life if all the villains wore black hats. My mother always said that if I kept expecting the villains to announce themselves, I was going to get hurt. She might not be right about many things, but she was right about that."

I definitely regretted inviting the crazy, semi-raving pregnant girl into the house.

"I don't know what you're talking about," I said.

"But even villains have mothers," she mused as if I hadn't spoken. She looked at me, as if looking for conformation on my villainess or maybe some indication that I did, in fact, have a mother. "Somewhere in you there has to be a kernel of understanding and decency."

"I don't really know—" I started again.

She interrupted. "I am Olivia Weiss."

She said her name as if it should mean something to me.

It didn't.

"I came here today to tell you to leave Alan Thompson alone. We're engaged and planning to get married soon. But you have to know that. I don't know how you can live with yourself. Really, I don't."

I knew what her words implied, but I didn't want to believe. Couldn't believe.

"Wait. You're having a baby?" I asked dumbly because it was obvious she was indeed having a baby. The question was, "Whose baby?"

Now she was looking at me as if *I* were the crazy one. "Alan's of course."

The small, perfect world I'd worked so hard to build for my family shattered in that moment. I looked at the girl...

Yes, she was no more than a girl in her mid-twenties to my thirties. A young woman who wore her anger and indignation like a mantle.

"Olivia," I started.

I wanted to hate her, this girl-woman. She'd barged into my home and shattered the perfect life I thought I had. But from her comments I knew she didn't know who I was. And with perfectly clear insight that seemed out of place given my muddled emotions, I knew that Alan had lied to her just as he'd lied to me. There was no way to hate her for that. "I'm—"

"Mom," Jeremy hollered as he thundered down the wooden staircase. "Haley took my hockey pucks. All of them. She says she's holdin' them for ratsom—"

"*Ransom*," Haley corrected him with the smugness of a younger sister correcting an older brother.

"Yeah, *ransom*. She says I can't have 'em back unless I come to her stupid tea party."

"We don't use the word stupid here," I corrected without thinking.

This was normal. The kids tattling and spatting was part of my normal, *perfect* life.

That life had been shattered for me, but I knew I needed to protect the kids. "I think you two should work this out for yourselves. Haley, we don't hold other people's things for ransom and Jeremy, I'm pretty sure Haley played hockey with you last night. It might be time to do something she enjoys."

"Yeah, that's only fair," Haley informed her eight-year-old brother. She was seven and I knew she resented being the younger sibling. It felt as if she'd been born trying to catch up to Jeremy. She walked at ten months and ran minutes later.

She'd been running after her older brother ever since.

"Upstairs," I said. "Work it out and don't come down until I call you."

They trudged up the stairs, muttering to each other.

Their unity against me had ended their quarrel.

I turned to look at Olivia. She was white as a sheet.

"That was Alan's son," she managed.

I nodded. Jeremy was the spitting image of his father.

"So," she said slowly, as if trying to come to terms with what she'd just discovered. "So, *I am* the other woman?"

Some women, given her condition, would swoon or at least bend beneath the pain of what they'd just learned.

Olivia Weiss was not some women. She held herself ramrod straight as the reality of what she'd just learned sank in.

"*I am the other woman*," she said firmly.

Yes, some women would hate this usurper—this young woman who had shattered their fairytale life.

But I couldn't hate her.

I felt a connection with her.

We were two women who'd thought we'd found the love of our lives ... with the same man.

"You didn't know," I stated, not asked.

She shook her head, her hands resting on her huge stomach.

Then it hit me—she was carrying my children's sibling.

If Alan were here, I'd gladly ...

I'm not sure what I'd do to him. Jeremy would probably have some inventive torture, but I was at a loss.

This morning, I'd have said I'd have done anything *for* Alan. But at this moment, I was pretty sure that I could do anything *to* Alan.

"Take off your coat and come sit down. Alan will be home soon and I have a lot to say to him. I suspect you might have a thing or two to say as well."

I sounded calm to my own ears. I'm not sure why or how.

"You're inviting me in instead of kicking me to the curb?" she asked.

Despite the fact my world was crashing down, I found myself nodding.

"The way I see it—not that I've had much time to digest this." That was an understatement if ever there was one. "But then neither have you. As I see it, this whole thing is on Alan. I don't know you and you don't know me, but we didn't do this." I waved my hands between us.

I paused a moment, then added, "I can assure you that I will be kicking *him* to the proverbial curb."

Alan Thompson.

My high school sweetheart.

The man I'd promised to spend my life with.

The man I'd promised to love forever.

I was kicking him out.

"Maybe you'd rather not be here," I said. "I mean, maybe you want him—"

She scoffed and sounded decades older than she looked. "You're right, you don't know me and I don't know you, but I would rather move back home with my family than take Alan back. And since you don't know me, I'll tell you that moving back home is the absolute last thing in the world I'd ever do. I'd prefer being pregnant for years. I'd rather ... I'd rather ..."

She'd run out of awful comparisons, but I got it.

"It's been a rough pregnancy," she added. "I don't want to be pregnant one more minute, but..."

Someone who'd never had a child might not understand the enormity of what she was saying, but I did.

"Would you rather let him know that you know privately?" I asked.

She shook her head. "No. I think I prefer seeing his expression when he walks in and finds the two of us here together."

She took off her coat. I realized that I should have taken it from her, but she was already taking the seat I offered and placed her coat on the chair behind her.

So I sat as well and I tried to decide how to make small talk with my husband's mistress. "When is the baby due?"

The baby, who would be Jeremy and Haley's sibling.

I was done having children. Two was plenty, both Alan and I agreed. And yet, here he was, having a third child.

I waited for the pain to hit me. It was there. A tiny bubble that was building deep within my core. When the pressure grew too great, it would burst and I'd be incapacitated by it. But I wasn't willing to let it burst yet.

I pushed it aside for the moment.

Again with absolute clarity I knew that the perfect life I thought I'd built wasn't perfect at all. And I knew this wasn't what I wanted.

I wondered what I did want, but knew I wouldn't find an answer now.

Olivia said, "The baby will be here soon. Any day according to the doctor."

We both sat in awkward silence. I knew she had to be hurting as much as I was.

How could Alan do this to me?

To her?

To our kids?

To her baby?

"How did you find out about me?" I finally asked.

"Alan's cellphone rang and when he looked to see who was calling he sent the call straight to voicemail rather than pick up. He looked at me..." She shrugged. "I don't know how to describe it, but I knew. I just knew. So later, I snooped."

She shook her head and her hair tumbled back and forth across her shoulders. "I never thought I'd be *that* woman," she said softly. "I always looked down on people who snuck around checking up on a significant other—looking at their email or cellphones. If someone had asked me before that moment, I'd have said my relationship with Alan was based on trust. I would have been so smugly confident in what we had. And still, I snooped. When I did, I saw your name. You have a different last name than him, so I assumed..."

"I kept my last name when we married. We hyphenated the kids' last names." And suddenly I wondered if I'd known even then there was a chance we might not last. I'd always known that Alan was weak, but not in this way. Not a cheater.

Olivia nodded even as her eyes welled up with tears. "Your last name was different, so I assumed you were a mistress. I didn't want to believe it. I listened to the voicemail. You asked him to grab a gallon of milk and some bread just in case the storm was as bad as they said and you got snowed in. Then you said, *love you.* It was casual and almost an afterthought. *Love you.*"

Had it been casual?

Had I treated our love as if it were mundane?

Love should never be an afterthought. It should be a first thought and a second thought... and finally a last thought.

Olivia looked as if she wanted to cry, but like me, she tamped down her tears. She squared her shoulders and said, "I was thinking that it would be nice if all the bad guys had to wear black hats. Yet, when you opened the door, you looked nice and then the kids…" She paused. "I realized I was the one who should have had a black hat."

"You do realize what color hat you had on?" I asked and started to laugh at the thought of her black knit hat.

She paused a moment and realized that she had indeed been wearing a black hat. She started to laugh as well.

It wasn't really funny, but somehow laughing eased that bubble of pain for the moment.

That's how Alan walked in … to the sound of us laughing.

And when he saw the two of us he stood absolutely still.

I've heard the term *a-deer-in-the-headlights*. I never really understood exactly what it meant until that moment.

"I…" That's all he said.

Really what more could he say?

I'd been with him long enough to be able to hear his inner debate. Which of us should he try to appease?

"Alan, I think it would be for the best if you packed up a bag and went somewhere, anywhere, but here. Now. For good. I'll go see a lawyer tomorrow. I don't know what the requirements are in Pennsylvania, but as soon as we legally can, we're divorcing. We'll split our assets fairly. You'll have access to our kids and I will never badmouth you to them. I'd appreciate if you'd agree to the same. And other than finalizing the divorce and working out things for the kids, we're done."

"I want to explain," he started.

Olivia cleared her throat and he looked at her.

"We were engaged and talking about getting married next year," she said. "How could you have led me on? How could you have turned me into the other woman? You know how I feel about that," was all she said before she started to cry.

"Go pack a bag," I told him. "Tell the kids goodnight and get out. I'll contact you tomorrow with a lawyer's name."

"I—" he said again, then looked at us both and simply walked out of the room and up the stairs.

"Alice," Olivia said in a soft whisper. "Just to really make sure this night is forever imbedded in our memories, I think I'm in labor."

There are two ways to handle a stressful situation—with tears or laughter. Olivia went the second way and my laughter joined hers.

"Are they bad?" I asked.

She shook her head. "No. I'll call the doctor when Alan's left. I know it's mean, but I don't want him with me."

It wasn't as mean as she thought. Alan had never come in with me when I had the kids. He told me he'd be worthless with all the *mess*.

Tonight he'd shown how utterly worthless he was.

"I'll call the neighbor to come stay with the kids and drive you to the hospital if you'd like," I offered.

"You'd do that?" she asked.

"Of course." And I meant it. I know some women might hate Olivia. They might try to blame her, if only to make it possible to overlook their husband's indiscretion.

I wasn't that kind of woman.

As far as I was concerned, Alan had shown his true colors . . . and his colors happened to clash with mine.

"You're a nicer woman than Al deserved," Olivia said.

"So are you," I told her.

Olivia had just finished riding out another contraction when Alan came down the stairs, overnight bag in hand. He looked as if he planned to say something, but we both started to laugh again. His expression was somewhere between shocked and embarrassment.

I looked at him—the ratfink man I thought I'd spend the rest of my life with—and said, "This is every man's worst nightmare, his wife and mistress getting together. But hold on, Alan, because you know what's even worse? I think I really like her."

"Ditto," she said.

And we both collapsed into laughter as Alan walked out of the house.

Neither of us mentioned there might have been something more than mirth involved.

Chapter One

Alice
Two Months Later

On the plus side: You don't have to grow up
with a sibling in order to have a sister.

"What do you think?" I asked Olivia as we stood on a snowy sidewalk, staring at a large home on Front Street. It was a neighborhood in flux. The new bayfront development was down a huge cliff to the north. There were only houses on the south side of the street and all of them had a great view of the bay.

If I turned around and looked to the north, I knew I could make out the Convention Center that sat up against the bay. I'd be able to see the outline of Presque Isle, the peninsula that sat on the far side of the bay.

But I was looking south at the house.

It was an older home. It had white siding and black shutters. There was a huge porch with two doors.

"Gentrification," I said, more to myself than Olivia.

"What?" Olivia asked.

"This neighborhood is being gentrified, one house at a time. I'm getting in on the ground floor. I know it needs work," I continued quickly, "but it's close to the hospital, and the views from the upstairs bedrooms are amazing. Each unit has one bathroom, three bedrooms and when we're done with the renovations, we each can have an open concept downstairs."

"You're sure?" she asked.

In the two months since Olivia had entered my home, we'd become allies. I wasn't sure how it happened. I'd stayed with Olivia when she gave birth. I drove her home from the hospital. And it seemed natural to take her over dinner the next week. And of course, I'd held the baby.

The next time I visited, I'd taken the kids. I'd explained that their Dad and Olivia had a baby and she was their sister.

They were still torn up about Alan leaving, but thankfully, they didn't ask why their father didn't live with Olivia, and they were too young to understand the timeline of pregnancy. They accepted the baby was *theirs*. And once they knew, they wanted to see her often.

Alan was supposed to have the kids on nights I worked, but one night he flaked a half an hour before I had to leave for the hospital. I called Olivia.

I offered to take the baby the next week on a day off so she could work in peace and quiet.

Gradually, Alan took the kids less and less, which meant Olivia and I filled in more and more.

This move made sense.

"Each house has a downstairs and upstairs," I said. "We just share one wall. But since I have to do renovations, I thought we could have doors put in on the inside. Sort of like a hotel room. They would lock on both sides, but if you're watching my kids, or I'm watching Charity we could leave them open. I checked and we can put one downstairs in the living rooms and there's a hall linen closet upstairs that I think we can blow out and make a door upstairs between the halls."

"What will Alan say?" Olivia asked with a laugh. Alan was already befuddled by our friendship.

"Whatever he thinks doesn't matter to me."

"Me either," she said. "It would have to be on the condition that I pull my own weight financially."

I felt relieved, not that she was offering to pay her own way, but because she was saying yes.

"Of course," I quickly agreed.

"And you stop apologizing when I fill in because Alan leaves you high and dry," she added.

"Only if you stop apologizing for me taking the baby in the afternoons. The kids love their sister, and I'll confess, I may have fallen under her spell, too." I'd bought my own car seat and simply took the baby with me to pick the kids up from school and to do any errands that needed done on days I had her.

She was one of those dream babies who pretty much just went with the flow.

"No one will understand this," Olivia said. "I'm not sure I do."

"If I'm honest, neither do I. But I know that I like you. And I adore Charity as much as her big brother and sister do. And most importantly, neither of us did anything wrong."

I'd sold my perfect house in its perfect neighborhood. We were closing in a month. There was a lot to do before then.

I'd never bought a house on my own. And Alan wouldn't like this house. He'd feel it was too small and he'd never want to share a house with someone else. But this could work.

It could be a solution for both Olivia and me.

We could trade off babysitting by simply opening a door.

Olivia turned from the house and looked at me. "I don't see how you can not be bothered by Charity. She looks like Alan and that has to be—"

I interrupted her. "That's not what I see."

"What do you see?" Olivia asked slowly.

"When I look at Charity, I see the baby I helped bring into this world. I see Jeremy and Haley's sister. She looks like Jeremy did. I see that and remember when he was little."

"What do you see when you look at me?" Olivia asked softly.

"I see someone who was lied to. I see someone who had her world turned upside down and has dealt with everything with grace."

I paused. "And... I don't know how to put this. I believe there are relationships that are meant to be. Not romances, though I'm sure those count. I'm talking people who come into our lives at the right moment and change things for the better. You and me? I think we were destined to be... allies? Friends? Something. I know that rather than a painful reminder of Alan's infidelity, you and Charity are a comfort."

She brushed at her eyes. "And you're sure you want to share a house with us? We'll be outnumbered you and me. Three kids and two adults. Those are tough odds."

I laughed. "I think we've both proven we're tough enough to handle those odds and anything else that comes our way. And I think for right now, it would be a perfect situation for both of us. If you're willing, you could help with the kids on the nights Alan can't... or won't. And during the day, I'll keep taking Charity. It's not conventional, but..." I shrugged.

Maybe this was too farfetched. "Listen, I get it if you—"

I didn't finish the sentence because Olivia was hugging me. "Thank you. My family... Well, let's just say I've never felt I had anyone who was always in my corner... until you."

I patted her back. "The contractor is coming over tomorrow, so let's go take a look and make some plans."

"I've never got to really design a house the way I want."

"I might be buying the house, but you have carte blanche on your side. You can set things up however you want."

And then Olivia gave a small squeak of happiness and actually rubbed her hands together. "Let's go."

I laughed and followed her.

This neighborhood was not like our Frontier Park neighborhood, but it was far more practical on my paycheck. With my half of the proceeds from our old house and rent from Olivia, it was definitely in my budget.

And it was a blank slate.

Suddenly I was as excited as Olivia was at that thought.

"Definitely let's start planning."

Chapter Two

Alice
Nine Months Later

On the plus side: Mothers learn to appreciate quiet moments.
For single mothers, they're even sweeter.

Seven P.M. to seven a.m. is a brutal shift.

I stood at the small coffee counter, waiting while my reward for a long night's work finished perking.

Yes, I was going to sit at the small table in the far corner for fifteen entire minutes and just enjoy the peace and quiet.

I put that on my plus side and started working on the rest of my morning's list.

On the plus side, I was going to have fifteen minutes that I was going to call my own.

On the plus side, working three twelve-hour shifts a week counted as fulltime employment at the hospital which meant full benefits.

On the minus side, twelve hours is a long shift, especially when you're working with critical care patients.

On the plus side, I have dinner with my kids every night.

On the minus side, when I clocked out, one of my patients was on his way to the OR for more surgery.

On the plus side, my other patient was moving down to the cardiac unit.

And on the plus side, my ex was taking the kids tonight. They were excited to spend time with him and I was excited about having a night off.

What on earth was I going to do? Maybe a bubble bath in a quiet, silent house?

It didn't matter what I did ... the plusses won.

"You're smiling," said a man who was behind me in line.

Well, it wasn't much of a line since it was just the two of us.

Normally, I was the only one waiting for the coffee shop to open. Seeing someone else was rare ... talking to someone else was rarer still.

I hefted my gym bag.

"Sorry," the man said. "I didn't mean to startle you. You were just standing there looking so serious and then suddenly you smiled."

I looked at him. I mean really looked. Not just that quick little gaze that people tended to use.

He had dark hair that seemed like it wanted to curl. He'd put something on it so it didn't. He had very blue eyes. People probably didn't notice that right off because they were hidden beneath glasses, but once I had noticed, I couldn't unnotice them.

What was he talking about? Oh, me smiling.

"I smiled because the *plusses* won out this morning," I said and realized it wasn't much of an answer. I could see the question in his eyes.

I was thinking about how to clarify my answer without sounding like a loon, when Serena handed me a small black coffee without my ordering it. I put my money on the counter.

"Have a good one," I told her, then I nodded to Mr. Blue Eyes, so he knew he was included.

"You, too, Sugar," Serena said.

"Oh you know I will." I took my coffee to *my* table and sat down.

The good thing about the first one in line every morning was I didn't have to compete for a seat.

This was the perfect place to sit back and watch the hospital lobby come to life. Employees on their way into work, others leaving work and heading home. Some I knew, most I didn't. It was a big complex and I worked in a small, highly specialized unit so there were more of the latter than the former.

I watched patients on their way in. Families. And—

"The plusses won?" the guy who'd been behind in me in line asked as he sat down at my table.

Uninvited.

I waited to feel annoyed that he was interrupting my precious quiet minutes, but for some reason, annoyance wasn't what I felt.

Mr. Blue Eyes took a sip of his still scalding coffee and waited for an explanation.

For some unknown reason, I found myself answering him. "Life is full of ups and downs, good and bad. I like to look at what's going on in my life and put things in a plus column and a minus column. I smiled because this morning, the plusses won."

"Okay, that makes sense," he said. He didn't give me that she's-crazy look. "Do the plusses win a lot?"

"Can I tell you a secret?" I asked in a mock-whisper.

He nodded.

"I stack the deck," I admitted. "It's a rare day that the plusses don't win because even if the day's been a series of disasters, I can always find something for the plus column."

"Such as?" he asked.

"This is a ridiculous conversation," I said, knowing that all the ridiculous elements were my fault. But I spent a twelve-hour shift being totally serious. I guess I deserved a bit of ridiculous. So I answered, "A cup of hot coffee can always go on the plus side."

As if on cue, a mother walked in with a toddler in her arms. I'm not sure what she said, but the little girl giggled, which made me smile. "A child's laugh—plus."

He considered it for a moment and then nodded. "That does put a nice spin on a day."

"It does," I agreed.

He extended his hand. "Callum."

I didn't take his hand in mine, but I nodded and said, "Alice."

"What do you do, Alice?"

I could have answered that I was a charge nurse on the ICU floor.

Or I could have said that I was a divorced mother of two.

If I'd been wearing my scrubs, he might have guessed the first part. But I'd stopped at the hospital's gym and grabbed a shower. In yoga pants and a t-shirt, I could be anyone. I could work at any job. I could be an employee of the hospital, or a family member of a patient, or a patient myself for that matter.

The fifteen minutes I allowed myself for a cup of coffee in the morning was really my only time to breathe all day. I didn't want to give up those precious few minutes that comprised my break from the reality of my busy life, so I answered, "Captain Alice of the Starship USS Glass-Half-Full. Our five year mission is to travel the universe searching for absurd bits of happiness wherever we can find them."

Callum didn't seem to mind my irreverent answer. He quirked his eyebrow and said with mock sincerity, "Captain Alice, maybe you're new to our planet, but hospitals aren't normally where we find happiness. People who come here are sick, some dying."

"Oh, you're wrong. Many—most—of the patients leave here healthier than when they entered. And even in the midst of tragedy, there can be beauty."

I thought of Gray—Graham Grayson—who was leaving our unit today for the cardiac unit. "Maybe some young couple who suffered a loss came here. Maybe they thought their relationship was irrevocably broken."

"But it wasn't?" he asked.

I shook my head. "No. Maybe coming here made them remember what really matters."

"And that is?" he asked.

"Being there for each other. Saying the words that matter. Words like *love, I'm here* and *forgiveness*. Finding understanding."

"And you worked with such a couple?" he asked.

I shook my head and laughed. "No. I'm a starship captain, remember? I'm a collector of happy data. But stories like that are why hospitals can be a place where I can look for—and find—happiness."

What started out as a way to avoid answering his question left me feeling exposed. "Well, on that very odd note, I should go."

"You never answered my question," he said.

"Sure I did. I'm Alice. Just Alice."

Maybe that's why I didn't tell him I worked here. For the last few silly minutes, I'd been just Alice, a science fiction lover who tried to find the bright side of things.

I wasn't Alice, whose husband cheated on her.

I wasn't Alice a mom or Alice a nurse.

I was just Alice.

"Could I get your number, just Alice?"

Once I might have said yes, but frankly, the fifteen minutes I stolen from my morning were all the stolen moments I could manage. I didn't have time to date.

I shook my head and said, "Telephone signals can't reach our ship. Talk about bad reception. But thank you for..." What should I call what had just happened?

Suddenly, I knew. "Thanks for being another item in the plus column."

And I left quickly before he could ask me any more personal questions.

On the plus side, sharing coffee with a cute guy.

On the plus side, being just Alice again for just a few minutes.

Chapter Three

Olivia

On the plus side: I can't change the past and I can't see the future,
but I'm in total control of the present.

My house was clean. On the rare nights Alan had the kids, I ran around like a maniac getting things done. The house was small enough that getting things done didn't take very long.

I'd lived in a number of apartments since leaving my parents house. But no place had ever felt as much like home as this small duplex.

Alice had been true to her word. I chose every detail of the renovations. The entire downstairs was an open space. Unlike Alice, who liked to cook, I put in a small, eat-in kitchen to the back of house. The table was more often a workspace than a place for fine dining. There was a long island between the kitchen and the rest of the downstairs. I'd bought some funky stools and that was where I ate and where the kids sat on nights Alice worked and I had them.

She left after dinner, so all I ever provided was snack food and breakfast.

I might not be much of a cook, but it turns out that on the plus side: I'm very good at bedtime snacks and breakfast cereal.

I smiled at the thought.

Alice played the Plus-Side game with herself and I'd tried play as well. And like Alice, I tried to stack the deck, but I didn't find it quite as easy to do as she seemed to.

I took my coffee and went out on the front porch, waiting for Alan and the baby.

I could see the bay, and beyond it, the peninsula, Presque Isle State Park.

Alice and I had taken the kids to the park's beaches this summer. We generally went after supper, when worries about crowds and sunscreen diminished. The baby loved to sit in the shallows and try to eat stones. Haley and Jeremy would run around splashing each other or building sandcastles.

One evening, I'd heard Alice whisper, "On the plus side."

I asked her about it and that's when she explained her game.

As I stood on the porch, I could smell the water. I could hear the seagulls crying as they careened overhead. I could also make out the faint whoosh of the Bayfront Highway's traffic, though the bluff blocked my view of the cars.

"On the plus side: this view."

I caught myself saying the words out loud and smiled.

Alice was rubbing off on me. And I realized that was definitely a plus-side thing.

That night when I came to her Frontier Park home, all indignant and self-righteous, she'd taken me into her home and later, taken me to the hospital. That was truly going above and beyond.

But then she stayed.

She'd held my hand and cheered me on.

And when Charity was born, she'd held her and whispered, "What a beautiful, bitty thing you are."

We'd all called Charity Bitty ever since.

This wasn't the life I'd planned, but it was a good life.

My plus-sides almost always outnumbered my minus-sides.

As if on cue, Alan pulled up in front of the house.

He was someone who was in the minus column most of the time, but I tried to be Alice-like and made myself think, *On the plus side: he'd had all three kids overnight.* And when a small voice whispered it was the first time in two weeks he'd seen any of the kids, I shushed it.

He'd dropped Haley and Jeremy at school, so he only had the baby in the car.

I hurried down as he got Bitty out of her car seat. She squealed when she saw me and I held her close. "Hey, Bitty Belle," I whispered as I kissed her baby-fat cheek.

Alan grumbled as he unhooked her car seat.

I'd told him it would be easier if he bought one and left it in the car. He'd told me he couldn't afford it.

Money was Alan's frequent complaint. He resented paying child support and was very vocal about how Alice and I were responsible for his less than solvent bank account.

At first I'd argued and pointed out that supporting his kids financially was the least he could do. But it was like talking to a wall.

I wondered if Alan had always been like that. Maybe being a professor had left him unable to see another side of an issue and learn something new.

Finally, he got the seat out, grabbed Bitty's bag and followed me into the house.

"How was she last night?" I asked as I took Bitty's shoes off and stripped her light jacket off her. The second I put her down, she shot from my arms at a very fast crawl to her toy box. I knew that my clean house was about to revert to its normal toy cluttered state.

As much as I liked having things neat and tidy, having Bitty home wreaking havoc was another big plus-side.

"My mother had a blast with the kids," he said.

I tried to give Alan the benefit of the doubt and believe he would have taken the kids if his mother hadn't come to town. But I had noticed that his infrequent times with the children corresponded to his mother's visits.

I sighed.

"When is she going to sleep through a night?" Alan grumbled. "I've got class at eleven and I'm going to be lucky to get through it."

I didn't mention that to date he'd only had Bitty twice overnight, and rarely more than a couple hours a week.

"Anything else?" I asked.

He shook his head.

"You got Haley and Jeremy to school on time?"

"I'm not totally inept," he grumbled.

I just waited and finally he nodded.

"Do you have a day next week you want her and the kids? Alice said she texted you her schedule."

"I'm not sure I can make any of those days work," he said.

Of course not.

I tried to emulate Alice and bit down my irritation.

"Well, let us know," I said, and opened the door.

"I don't understand how you and Alice can be friends."

Frankly, neither could I, but her friendship was on my plus side every single day since we'd met. I never had a mentor—someone I wanted to emulate. My mother…well, I absolutely did not want to grow up and be like my mother.

But Alice, though she was only a decade older, was someone I truly wanted to model myself after.

"I'm sure you don't," I said to Alan who was not moving toward the door.

Bitty got her bus-riding toy out and used it as handhold as she stood. "Be careful," I called out. She had a tendency to fall when she pushed it too fast. She'd be walking unaided soon.

Alice and I both agreed life would definitely be more interesting then.

"I don't understand why you moved here."

I smiled. "Again, I'm sure you don't."

"You have definitely been spending too much time with Alice. You sound just like her. I never understood how a woman could fight without ever raising her voice or saying a negative thing."

"She is an amazing woman," I replied.

Alan frowned and finally took my very broad hint and stormed out the door.

"If you find a day that seeing your children would be convenient, you just let us know, Alan," I called out before I shut the door.

Bitty had abandoned the bus and had proceeded to dump out a box of blocks.

There was a soft knock on the door that separated Alice's side of the house from mine. We both had locks, but I don't think either of us had ever used them.

"Come in," I called.

Alice opened the door looking totally Alice-like. She had on yoga pants, a tank top and a flannel shirt. Her hair was wrapped in a messy, wet bun and she had a mug in her hand.

I didn't need to ask to know the mug contained very hot, very black coffee.

On nights she worked, she stopped for coffee before coming home. She'd told me once that she felt guilty about it.

That summed up Alice's character as far as I was concerned. She was someone who felt taking fifteen minutes three times a week to herself was being self-indulgent.

"Good morning," she called to Bitty, who ran to Alice. She set her coffee down and opened arms as she scooped Bitty up.

"I'm going to admit, I was a coward and didn't come over when I saw Alan. How was last night?" she asked me as Bitty proceeded to babble at Alice.

"I think one of the beauties of our relationship is being able to split up our dealings with Alan," I said with a laugh.

Alice, Bitty still in hand, sat on the couch. "Thanks for letting me off the hook."

"He said *his mother* really enjoyed the kids last night."

She laughed. "Just as we suspected. Helen was never overly fond of me, but she truly loves the kids. Did he say if he wants the kids again any time soon?"

"He was decidedly uncertain," I said. Ready to turn the subject to something more pleasant, I asked, "Why are you up so early?"

Working three twelve-hour night shifts a week left Alice with decidedly odd sleep patterns. It worried me. I might be sleep deprived from getting up with the baby, but it was nothing to having to rotate a sleep cycle on a nightly basis.

Bitty squirmed out of Alice's lap and went back to her toys.

"I have no idea why I'm up so early. I woke up and the sun was shining. I tried to go back to sleep, but I couldn't. So I thought I'd see if Bitty would like to go for a long walk with me? I'll feed her lunch and bring her back just in time for a nap. That should give you a few hours to work in peace and quiet."

I nodded. "That sounds great."

"Wonderful. I'll come back in about fifteen minutes to pick her up."

She grabbed her coffee, took an unbelievably long sip and hurried back through the door. She didn't bother shutting it.

Bitty tore through the books off her shelf. She found the one she wanted, and held it out to me.

"That's a good one."

I happily picked my daughter up and started reading, Fi Fly Flo for the hundredth time. Bitty reached up and grabbed a strand of my hair in one hand, holding it like a security blanket, as she snuggled closer.

This was definitely a plus-side moment.

Chapter Four

Alice

On the plus side: Being a woman of mystery is so much more interesting than being the single mother of two ... and a half.

$\mathcal{I}$ was not the first person in line for coffee on Friday morning. That was almost unheard of.

On occasion, a patient's family would stumble down from their room and beat me to the counter, but that was rare.

I was pretty sure who was in line as I approached. He could be a patient's family. Heck he could be a patient or a fellow employee. We hadn't gone any further than names.

And frankly, that was as far as I'd wanted to go.

I could tiptoe and leave. He'd never know I'd been here.

But at the moment, he turned around and smiled as he saw me. And I knew I was smiling back at him as I said, "Good morning."

"I thought maybe I'd dreamed you up."

"Nope." I would have corrected one of the kids if they'd answered me like that, so I smiled and said, "I'm only here a few days a week."

"What—"

I wasn't sure if he was going to ask what for or what I did here, but I knew I didn't want to answer either. Serena handed both of us a coffee without asking. I handed her my money, so did Callum.

He nodded to my table and quirked his eyebrows, asking to join me without really asking. I found myself nodding, even though I wasn't sure I wanted to share a coffee with a man who under other circumstances I might have liked a lot.

We took the seats we'd had on Tuesday and I thought he'd ask his question again, but instead he said, "Which is winning today? Plusses or minuses?"

"Oh, plusses for sure," I assured him.

"So what's in the plus column?" he asked.

"I saw the newest Quentin Tarantino movie with a friend this week. She's a huge fan." QT, as Olivia called him, was not a child-friendly moviemaker, so we'd watched it one night when Alan had taken the kids. We'd ordered in Thai food and opened a bottle of wine.

It had definitely been a plus sort of night.

"And you're not a fan?" he asked.

"I find his movies a bit too violent for my taste. I always tell my friend that I feel as if I'm watching half the movie with my eyes shut. But since she's made me watch all of them, I've learned to appreciate the way he tells a story. I like them despite the violence, not because of it. We watched an interview with him a while back, and I have to say he'd be fascinating to visit with over a coffee."

"It's only our second date and I'm already being replaced by a movie star," Callum said with mock-dejection.

Rather than laugh, his words caught me unprepared. "This isn't...I mean, I can't—"

"Coffee date, not like going out sort of date," Callum said, reassuring me, though he gave me a look that said my reaction had taken him by surprise.

My panic at his choice of words took me by surprise as well.

I let out a breath slowly. "I don't want to lead you on. I can't date."

"Married?" he asked.

I snorted and shook my head. "Once, but not now. No significant other, either. The rest is personal."

"I get it. I date, but never..."

His sentence faded as I held up my hand. I realized that I didn't want to date him, but I had enjoyed having coffee with him and wouldn't mind sharing a morning coffee with him again.

I wasn't sure it was wise, but I still found myself saying, "Listen, I really enjoyed having coffee with you, but if we continue to see each other down here, I think we need ground rules."

"Such as?" he asked.

"I won't ever expect you and you won't expect me. But when we do run into each other, and if we share a coffee, it isn't romantic and it won't become romantic. We are just two people who are sharing a coffee and some of the plusses from our lives. Generic plusses. Nothing too personal."

"So you're not really a starship captain, but rather an international spy who has to be cautious forming personal attachments?" he teased.

International spy was so much more interesting than my real life so I smiled and nodded. "Something like that."

Callum held out his hand and shook mine. "Deal. So your plus was a movie with a friend. Mine was kayaking on Presque Isle lagoons this weekend. I spotted a bunch of..."

That was it. We talked about Presque Isle and Lake Erie. Before I knew it, my coffee was empty and I glanced at my watch. Twenty minutes.

I was five minutes over the time I normally allotted myself for my morning coffee.

"I hate to cut this short," I said, realizing it was very true, "but I have to run."

"Will I see you again?"

This was it. I could simply cut this off now and nip it in the bud. I could walk away and stop at Tim Horton's or Starbucks for a coffee tomorrow. That might be the wisest thing, but no one every accused me of being wise.

"I'll be here tomorrow," I said.

He nodded. "I'll see you then, if that's okay?"

"I'd like that as long as—"

I didn't need to finish. He made a scout sign and said, "I'm Callum, you're Alice and I'm going home to watch a Quentin Tarantino movie so we can discuss it."

I laughed as I smiled at my new friend. "Having a new coffee buddy is definitely my plus for today."

Then I left.

I think I smiled like a loon the entire ride home.

Olivia noticed when I checked in with her. She had the kids all at the counter eating breakfasts. I walked by all three of them, kissing the tops of their heads as I went down the line.

Olivia gave me an intense once over and finally said, "You look like the Cheshire Cat. Spill."

Olivia and I—strange as it seemed—had become more than friends or housemates. We were family. Our kids were family.

Alan was ... not.

When I kicked him out, I gave him open access to the kids, and so did Olivia, but he rarely took them.

Tuesday had been an exception and I wasn't surprised that it was because his mother was visiting. Helen and I had always gotten along, but we'd never been friends. I hadn't seen her since the separation.

And I didn't miss her.

But I would miss Olivia if she moved.

We'd become each other's back up. She watched the kids nights I worked, I took Bitty on days I was off or in the afternoons after I'd slept on days I worked.

Olivia was a translator. She spoke a lot of languages and translated everything from scholarly texts to fiction for a living. It turns out that babies were not overly conducive to such work.

It worked well when we traded babysitting. We both had our own space, but the door was there whenever we wanted to open it. Which was most of the time.

The renovations had turned out beautifully. I was amazed at how different our sides turned out. Her décor was country sleek. Even her paint seemed to scream style. It was an ice blue I'd have never thought of using. For furnishings, she'd used eclectic mix of antiques and new furniture that worked. My side was not quite country, nor sleek in the least. It was comfortable. I chose big overstuffed furniture and soothing autumnal colors.

"Alice?" Olivia prompted.

"I took an extra minute for coffee," I confessed. "I'm sorry."

"Stolen moments are the best kind of time," she assured me.

"Are you two almost ready to go?" I asked the kids. I didn't want to talk about Callum and our stolen moments.

Olivia knew almost everything about me by now and there was a comfort in having someone who knew you and liked you anyways. She was a bit more closemouthed about her past and family, but I felt as if I knew all the things that mattered.

Callum knew next to nothing about me and I was discovering there was a comfort in that as well.

"I forgot I need a shoe box," Jeremy said.

"How long have you known about it?" I asked.

He shrugged.

Now, something like that might seem like it should go in the negative column, but the fact he'd remembered before we were at the school's front door made it a positive. I wouldn't have to run home, get the box and then run back.

Olivia said, "I've got one I'm sure."

She left me with the kids as she ran to her room to get it.

She came back and handed me a designer brand shoebox.

I wanted to ask how a translator could afford Jimmy Choos, but I didn't. I suspected it was wrapped up with her parents, and from what little she said, her parents were difficult.

I loaded the kids in the car and we made it to school on time, with a shoebox and only one *he's-touching-me, she's-touching-me* fight.

That went on the plus side.

Seeing Callum again for coffee ... that was there, too.

Chapter Five

Alice

On the plus side: A stolen moment over coffee with a new friend.

$\mathcal{I}$was a few minutes late leaving the floor and I was surprised to discover I was anxious at the delay. I was afraid that Callum hadn't waited.

I thought about skipping a shower before going home, but I liked to leave the hospital germs at the hospital, so I simply made it a quick one.

By the time I hit the ground floor, I was prepared for solo coffee. I tried to tell myself that would be fine with me. I mean, Callum and I had only shared a couple cups of coffee.

He probably had better things to do than wait for someone who had made it clear this was nothing more than a coffee-friendship.

Yet, I was pleasantly surprised to find he was still there waiting for me ... at my table.

Maybe *our* table?

He handed me a coffee as I slid into a seat at the table.

"Thank you," I said. "I'm sorry I was late. This is going to be a fast coffee for me."

He nodded and jumped into a conversation with no pre-amble. "Plus side?"

I started to say having coffee with him, but that seemed too forward, so I settled for, "It was a quiet night last night."

He didn't ask why that was a plus or what normally made my nights anything but quiet. Instead he asked, "Minus?"

I shook my head. At this moment, sitting at a table with Callum, I couldn't think of anything. "Let's concentrate on plus-ses. What's yours this morning?"

"Sitting here, having coffee with you," he said.

I paused, coffee cup halfway between my mouth and the table and set it down as he echoed the words I'd been thinking.

As if to take some weight off the words he'd just said, he hurriedly added, "So I watched *Kill Bill*. The movie was out of sequence. I wasn't sure how I felt about it, and then..."

As he wound down, I admitted that at the end of the second film, I was hoping that The Bride didn't kill Bill after all.

"Did she?" he asked.

That awkward moment when I'd first sat down was forgot-ten as I teased, "You'll have to watch and find out."

"If she doesn't, what's the point of the title?" he asked.

"Maybe irony?" I asked.

He shook his head. "No, I'm pretty sure Bill's got to die."

A woman walking by our table must have overheard Callum's comment because she turned around and retraced her steps, heading for seats on the opposite end of the area.

I burst out laughing.

So did Callum.

"You'd best watch out," I warned him. "That is how people get a reputation."

We went back to our discussion, and when I glanced at my phone and saw the time, I was shocked at how quickly it had flown.

"I've really got to run," I said.

"Tomorrow morning?" he asked.

"I won't be back until Tuesday," I said.

He didn't ask questions. He simply smiled. "I'll see you then, if that's okay?"

I didn't have to think about my answer. I quickly nodded and said, "Let's just go with the assumption it's okay from now on. I'll tell you if that changes."

He shot me an impish grin. "I'll be on my best behavior."

I snorted, indicating I doubted he was ever on his best behavior.

He didn't take offense, but rather tried to look innocent.

I laughed at his attempt. I wasn't buying it.

Callum walked with me toward the front door of the hospital.

"Do you have any plans for the weekend?" he asked. "I just got the newest Harry Dresden book and plan to spend tomorrow reading it."

"Just the normal weekend chaos for me," I said.

I didn't elaborate and he didn't ask me to.

When I got home I threw dinner in the crockpot, slept until four, then went to retrieve the kids from Olivia. We had dinner together at my place most nights. I was used to cooking for four, and even though Bitty made five, she didn't eat much.

It turned out, Olivia was many things, but a good cook wasn't one of them.

Heck, a mediocre old cook wasn't one of them.

She used the small dining room area in her section of the house as more of an office and toy room. If the kids had breakfast there, they sat at the island counter.

At my house, we used the table. I'd bought Bitty a high chair. Jeremy and Haley spent a lot of time laughing at her messy table manners. Tonight the baby had decided mashed up potatoes made for great body art.

The kids shrieked as Bitty smeared potatoes on her face and in her hair.

I smiled at Olivia.

Once upon a time, my life was orderly. Alan worked, while I took care of our big fancy house and the kids. And by *took care of the house*, I mean, I really tried to have a house that looked like a magazine centerfold. Everything had a place and that place was as cute as I could make it.

I thought about those glass jars that had chalkboard labels on them all lined up in my old pantry. It seemed like a lifetime ago. Back then my pantry had been a thing of beauty. I had a Pinterest Board dedicated to organizing things. *Organized Insanity* I'd titled it and felt witty.

I didn't have time to play on Pinterest now, but if I did, I'd name the board *Joyful Chaos*.

This new life I was building for the kids and myself—for Olivia and Charity as well—wasn't nearly as organized. The small three bedroom home was orderly, but it was a breeze to take care of because I'd downsized when we moved. It was comfortable more than organized.

I still used glass jars for storage in the pantry, but the labels went supremely unchalked. The way I looked at it now that the jars were glass so I could look at them and see what was what.

Yes, I was not nearly as Pinterest pretty around the house, but there was a lot of joy here.

I looked at Olivia. She had her long blonde hair in a braid today and looked even younger than she normally did. She was an amazing young woman. Explaining my friendship with my husband's ex-mistress and her daughter to anyone would be difficult. But friendship didn't need an explanation... neither did family.

When Olivia had a stomach bug last spring, I packed her and the kids up and went to the ER. I filled out the forms, but realized that if Olivia were incapacitated, I'd have had no legal standing for her or Charity, and vice versa.

We'd gone to a lawyer and had power of attorney papers drawn up for both of us afterward.

The papers gave us legal standing. I was her power of attorney and she was mine.

It takes nine month to carry a baby. It took us a lot less time than that to realize we were family.

The people at this table, laughing as Bitty tried to get a bite of potato into her mouth with a spoon, were my family.

The worst night of my life had led me here and *here* was a pretty good place to be.

"How about after dinner if we watch—"

"*Star Wars*," Jeremy bellowed.

We'd watched the original *Star Wars* trilogy at least a dozen times in the last year, but we all loved them. Bitty could *da da da da da da da dum* the theme song. We all agreed that it probably meant she was a musical prodigy.

I looked at Olivia who nodded. "Sounds like a plan."

After an hour of the movie, Olivia and Charity went across to their place. "Dinner at my house tomorrow," she said. "I have a new recipe."

I made old standbys, when there was a rare evening that Olivia cooked it was always something new.

"It looks simple enough that even I can't ruin it," she added.

Haley and Jeremy both looked at me and rolled their eyes, which made me smile.

"You three stop it. You'll have Charity thinking her mama can't cook," Olivia scolded.

"She can't," Jeremy whispered loud enough for Olivia to hear and start laughing with us.

"We'll be your guinea pigs," I assured her, trying to contain my laughter.

The kids and I made short order out of homework, baths and a quick game of *Life*. Well as quick as *Life* can be. Then we read a chapter of the first Harry Potter.

When they went to bed, I remembered another Harry.

The one that Callum had mentioned. I downloaded the first Harry Dresden novel on my Kindle and read until I couldn't keep my eyes open any longer.

My last thought of the day was, this wasn't the life I planned, but it was a good life.

A life I loved.

That went on my plus side.

At the tail end of that thought was another one. *I'd see Callum on Tuesday.*

That went on my plus side for sure.

Chapter Six

Alice

On the plus side: Getting his digits.

"I finished the first Harry Dresden novel," I said as I handed Callum a coffee.

I hadn't mentioned I was reading it because I wanted to surprise him.

"You ordered it?" He looked pleased. "I finished the newest one."

"So what did you think without giving away too much? I have a lot of books to read to catch up. It's a big series, but if the first one's any indication, I'm in for a treat."

"You are. I love the character. I'm trying to think of where the series started. Maybe I'll need to reread them so we can talk about them in depth. But ..."

I could hear his enthusiasm for the series as he talked about Harry and his pals. As I talked about the first book, I realized that Callum's enthusiasm was contagious.

I had genuinely enjoyed the first book and I'd already downloaded the second one, but even if I hadn't, I'd have kept reading the series simply to be able to talk about the books with Callum in the future.

I realized with a small shock, I was imagining a future of coffees with Callum. For the last ten months, when I thought of the future, it included my kids, Olivia, and Bitty. And now, here was Callum—a man I only knew by his first name—nudging his way into my future, even if it was only coffees in the morning.

"Are you a mass murderer?" he asked out of the blue.

I snorted a bit of warm coffee through my nose, which led to a fit of very inelegant coughing.

When I finally caught my breath, I answered, "No. Are you?"

"No," he said with a rueful smile. "I just wondered why there's the no personal information rule."

"I'm not sure it's a *rule*, per se, but..." I paused. "No, you're right. It is a rule. It's *my* rule."

I hadn't been able to control what happened when Alan cheated. And while my new life was a good one, it wasn't one I had planned. I'd sort of fallen into it.

But this—my weird friendship with Callum—I could control. I could set the boundaries and let it be only what I wanted it to be.

Maybe what I needed it to be.

I tried to think of a way to explain all that without sounding crazy.

"I'm not a mass murderer or any sort of illegal anything," I started. "I'm not married nor do I have a significant other. I don't date, not because I'm against dating, but because I don't have time. My life is crazy right now. I know everyone says that, but for me, at this point in my life, it's true. Before I met you, I allowed myself one cup of coffee on days I wo—" I started to say worked, but quickly changed it to "was here. I had fifteen minutes to sip my coffee before going back to the chaos. Since I've met you, I've stretched that time to almost a half hour some mornings."

I did the math in my head. "This is our ninth morning together. I enjoy our conversations. I enjoy talking to you about books and movies. I was even thinking about branching out into current affairs. For the half hour or less on the mornings we meet, I'm just Alice. I don't owe you anything. You don't owe me anything. Meeting you is simple and enjoyable. This half hour is time I claim as simply mine. I'm here sharing coffee and conversation with you because I want to. Maybe it's selfish of me or maybe its sanity. I'm thinking *sanity*. But I'm squeezing this time with you into a filled-to-the-brim day because I deserve thirty minutes out of the one thousand, four hundred and forty minutes each day to call my own."

He studied me for a moment and slowly nodded. "And if I said I'd like it to be more?"

I shook my head sadly. "I'd say I don't have time."

And suddenly I realized that I would miss Callum if he decided to say this was too weird.

More than that, I realized that I wished I *did* have time.

I felt stirrings of feelings I hadn't felt in … years.

Somewhere along the line, Alan and I had drifted apart.

I don't think I realized it until the moment Olivia showed up on my doorstep. And even then I don't think I'd realized how far apart we'd been. I hadn't realized until this moment as I sat looking at Callum and wishing there were more than twenty-four hours—more than one thousand, four hundred and forty minutes—in a day.

I wished I could lean across this table and kiss him. I'd like to be that bold and wild. I'd like to ask him to take me home with him.

"I wish this could be more," I admitted honestly. "But right now, this half hour a few days a week is all I can manage. And I'm sorry for that."

He studied me a moment, then nodded slowly.

I wasn't sure what that nod meant. "I can go if you—"

"No." He reached across the table and took my hand, as if to keep me from running away. "But I wondered if we could exchange cell phone numbers? Nothing more personal than that. We could text about books on days we can't meet. Maybe keep the same time frame. Over a cup of coffee in the morning. We can text and talk for a bit before we both jump into our real lives."

I could imagine myself getting up before the kids, starting my coffee and finding a text from Callum. Knowing that I wasn't going to lose this time with him, but in fact have more time with him made me feel so much lighter.

"I'd like that."

"And maybe someday, you'll share more about the real you."

"Callum, if I'm honest, I think I am doing just that here. You don't see me through any particular lens. You don't define me as part of my family, my job, or anything else. I'm just me. Just Alice. I think that's as real as I get."

He was thoughtful for a minute, then nodded. "Maybe you're right. So maybe that's another one of our rules? Always be real, whether we're talking about heavy things or minutia?"

"I like a man who uses the word *minutia*," I said as relief flooded through my body.

The next morning, at precisely seven my phone beeped.

Quiddity, he texted.

? I texted back.

You liked the word minutia, I thought I'd pull out another cool word that means essence. *That's what this morning is. So what about the book?*

I was still smiling over the word quiddity. *I read four chapters and would have kept reading, but I couldn't keep my eyes open.*

That's how it is whenever I read Butcher's stuff.

Is your coffee hot? I texted.

I stopped at the counter this morning and I'm sitting at our table. The coffee's hot, but it seems lonely without you. Serena asked where you were.

She did?

Where's your friend, is what she said.

I liked that. Friends.

My relationship with Olivia was more than a friendship. It came with the kind of strings that families have. Complex, a bit messy, but wrapped up with love.

With Callum, there was just friendship. Nothing complex or messy. Just coffee and camaraderie.

I didn't say that, instead I texted, *Did you see the weather report? Chance of snow for Halloween.*

Yes. Are you dressing up? he asked.

I'll see you for coffee on Halloween. I'll come in costume.

There was a long pause then he texted, *Can't wait. Gotta run. Talk to you tomorrow.*

I'll be here, coffee in one hand, the phone in the other.

Minutes after our last text, I finished my coffee and heard the kids charging down the stairs before I saw them.

I started my day with a smile and a big mark in my plus column.

I thought about costumes that I could manage at work.

Chapter Seven

Alice

On the plus side: Finding someone who shares your wavelength.

On halloween morning, I'd showered, put on my makeshift costume before I headed to the coffee shop. I was waiting at the counter when Callum came into view.

I didn't need an explanation for his costume. He was wearing a long, leather coat and hat. He was Harry Dresden.

"Harry," I called out as I laughed.

He noticed the Halloween skull on the neon orange t-shirt I'd borrowed from Olivia.

"Bob," he called back, referring to the fictional wizard's fictional sidekick, Bob the skull.

Serena laughed as well. "I'm a fan, Harry and Bob. And today's trick or treat is your coffee's on the house."

Callum dropped a ten in her tip jar and said, "Happy Halloween," before he followed me to our table.

We talked about Harry Dresden. Callum mentioned there had been a short-lived television series. He'd caught a few episodes. We decided we'd get the DVDs and watch it together.

I was about to leave for home when he said, "Happenstance."

"Pardon?"

"The word comes from the words happen and circumstance. I think it might be the perfect word for us."

"Meeting you was definitely a happy circumstance," I said. And then I leaned down and kissed his cheek.

I was as surprised as he seemed to be by my action. Not that he seemed upset. No he seemed a little bemused.

I kiss a lot of cheeks. My kids. Bitty.

Thinking of the baby wasn't enough to stop me from realizing this was something more than a kiss on a cheek should be.

I felt a buzz of awareness as I turned and left the table without waiting to see Callum's reaction.

I stepped outside the hospital and took a deep breath, trying to calm my racing heart.

My cellphone dinged and I automatically picked it up to check. It was Callum. All his text said was, *Definitely on the plus side.*

Chapter Eight

Alice

On the plus side: An evening of television with a friend.

I put together my requests for the December schedule the
night before. I did the math. This morning would be my
fifteenth actual meeting for coffee today with Callum. I'd met him
in October and it was November now.

Serena was doing a Thanksgiving dinner fundraiser. You
paid a dollar and got a cardboard leaf pasted to the wall behind
the counter. Callum and I donated every morning. After our
first leaf, we started putting them in fictional characters' names.
That's why Harry had a leaf, so did Bob and then I suggested we
branch out and added other fictional characters.

Serena said something about us not using our real names and
Callum told her that we didn't need a *plethora* of leaves. Then he
looked at me and we both laughed.

Serena smiled, not because she got why the word *plethora*
gave us so much glee, but because she liked us.

Callum and I texted a lot now.

At first it was just in the morning, during our normal coffee
time. But as the days went on, it became more frequent.

Callum was the first one I spoke to every day and the last one every night.

I wasn't always able to answer right away.

Frequently, I was sleeping when he texted and hours would go by. At first I turned off my phone when I went to sleep out of force of habit, and then I turned it off because I was afraid I'd wake up to read a text from him.

If I did that, then it would mean he'd become too much a part of the fabric of my life.

I could give him a small portion—the bits of time I allowed just for me I could share with him. But no more than that.

Olivia never asked who I was texting.

I might only see Callum three days out of seven, but it no longer felt like it. We watched shows at night. First *The Dresden Files*. We complained that it got canceled too soon.

Con Man was our new binge watch. We watched an episode each night after I tucked the kids in. They were all under a half hour. I could manage that.

We joked about the fact we were rather boring together.

We were simply two people who talked about books, movies and music.

Sitting with him at our table, sipping our coffee felt natural to me. Today we were talking about the *Star Wars Rebels* cartoon I'd watched with the kids. Callum had finally watched part of it last night.

"It was a good bridge between what happened after the original movies and what will come in the new ones. Maybe we could watch one together..."

He started, then let the sentence fade as I froze.

He sighed. "Alice, it's fine."

I forced myself to take a breath. "I know. Sorry. It's just that this is special. I know to someone on the outside looking in, it might seem boring—"

"Hey," Callum protested. "We are many things, but I don't think boring is one of them."

I smiled. He could protest, but I knew someone looking at us from the outside would see two exceedingly boring people.

We might talk about neighboring Panama Rocks, but we'd never go together.

We might talk about local restaurants or Erie's Presque Isle peninsula, but we'd never go to them either.

And I knew that it wasn't because of Callum. It was because of me.

How on earth could I explain my hesitancy to him when I could hardly explain it to myself?

I'd met Alan when I was young. I'd married him and had his children. I'd cleaned his house and washed his laundry.

I'd built my life around him.

We'd built a life together.

I thought it was a perfect life, but it had been built on a lie.

Because while I'd been doing all that, he'd been with other women.

Women plural.

I hadn't asked him, but I didn't need confirmation. I simply knew it.

From what I'd learned about him and Olivia, Alan was smooth. Too practiced.

He'd strung her along, dangling the idea of a more permanent relationship in front of her.

"Now, in honor of not being boring..." We spent the rest of our time talking about a cartoon.

"No we're not boring at all," I said as I gathered my coat and gym bag. "We're *scintillating*."

This time, Callum leaned forward and kissed me. I felt as awkward as a teenager afterwards.

"See you tomorrow," I mumbled as I beat a hasty retreat.

Chapter Nine

Alice

On the plus side: Non-mushy vegetables.

The next morning, I was the first one at the coffee counter. I got both our coffees, paid Serena for those and two more leaves. For names I used *Scintillating* and *Not-Boring*.

She held them up as Callum walked up to the bar. He laughed as I handed him his coffee.

Serena just shook her head and said, "You two aren't boring, but you are a bit weird."

That only made Callum laugh harder.

We sat at our table and he said, "Here's a question. Canned vegetables or frozen?"

"Pardon me?" I said.

"I had a debate with someone about which was more appetizing. We both agreed fresh was probably the way to go, but disagreed on what came second. So I'm asking you, frozen or canned?"

"Which did you choose?" I asked.

He shook his head and his glasses fell down the bridge of his nose. He pushed them back in place and said, "You answer first. I don't want to bias you."

"Frozen," I said.

"Frozen," he echoed.

I nodded. "Canned vegetables are just wrong. They're all mushy and soft. Except maybe mushrooms. I don't mind canned mushrooms. But if you think about it, they're on the mushy side of things when they're fresh."

He nodded his head toward the coffee counter. "You know how we agreed we weren't boring yesterday..." and just left the sentence hanging as he smiled.

"I don't think this is boring at all. I think those small things are what make us so interesting. Our likes and dislikes. Our interests. Maybe that's where so many couples go wrong. They talk about all the big things, but ignore *minutia*."

He smiled at the word, which had been my intent.

I continued, "Maybe they get so hung up on the big pictures, they ignore the small things that matter. Maybe if you take all those small things and string them together, you find it's a very big thing. A thing that's at our core."

He didn't look convinced.

"Have you ever studied art?" He shook his head.

"I took a couple classes in college. Pointillism is when artists like Seurat paint small individual dots of color and through those tiny spots they create an entire picture. Things like frozen vegetables and favorite movies are just dots that make the full picture of us."

Callum suddenly looked serious.

I felt a spurt of trepidation. "Callum—"

He shook his head and interrupted me. "I've enjoyed getting to know you through your *dots*, but Alice, I want more. I want to go out on a date. We can meet and have dinner together. You don't have to let me into the rest of your life yet, if you're not ready."

This had been nice... meeting Callum and not having any expectations. But he was right. Maybe it was time for more. I knew that Olivia would babysit if I went out with Callum and Alan wouldn't or couldn't take the kids.

I thought about dinner with him and then maybe afterwards a kiss. Something more private than our very public ones had been.

"I—"

"Mom," screamed a voice I recognized.

I turned and saw Olivia with Bitty on one hip and Haley on the other. Haley was holding a bucket.

Jeremy was running ahead calling me. "Mom, come on."

I got up, forgetting about Callum and questions of dating, as I rushed toward my family. "What happened?"

"She can't seem to stop throwing up. At first I didn't worry, but…" Olivia said as I grabbed Haley from her. "I'm afraid she'll dehydrate if she hasn't already."

I nodded. "Okay, let's go to the ER. I'm sure someone there will take a look."

I started towards the hall that would lead to the ER. Callum was suddenly by my side, handing me my bag.

"Do you need help?" he asked.

I shook my head. "No, I've got it. But thanks."

I turned and hurried down the hall I was so worried about Haley that it wasn't until later that night when Callum texted, *I hope your daughter was all right*, and I assured him that she was fine.

He didn't text anything back. I remembered the look he'd had when he spotted the kids and realized I was their mother.

It was a look that should have told me immediately that though he'd thought he wanted to know more about me, he'd just rejected the biggest part of who I was … a mother.

Well, that was fine. I'd let him into my life, but not too far into my life. Letting him go would be easy.

I was relieved that I'd never responded to his dinner invitation.

I'd been on the cusp of saying yes.

Chapter Ten

Olivia

Plus side "I never want to say the words, if only ..."

When I was in this hospital for Bitty's birth it had been one of the best days of my life.

And one of the worst.

It was the day I discovered that I was inadvertently a chip off the block. My father's block.

Not that being a chip off my mother's block would have been much better.

Any better.

Emerson and Pauline Weiss were blocks I didn't want to emulate.

"Aunt Olivia, when's Mom gonna come tell us about Haley?" Jeremy asked.

I patted the couch next to me and he sat close enough that our thighs touched. I wanted to reach out and hug him to me, but at nine Jeremy was too old for such things.

Of course, I hadn't known him before his father left, but the little boy I'd grown to know over the last eleven months was a serious child.

He was also Bitty's favorite person in the world. When I saw him patiently rolling a ball to her or reading her *King Bidgood's in the Bathtub* for the umpteenth time, I always melted just a little.

He might not be related to me by blood, but I couldn't have loved him any more if I'd given birth to him.

Same thing for Haley and Alice.

Trying to explain our connection to people was next to impossible, but it was there and it was strong. I'd thought about it a lot over the last few months, and I'd finally decided that I didn't need to explain myself to anyone else.

We were family. That's all anyone else needed to know.

I messed up Jeremy's hair in lieu of the hug I wanted to give him. "Honey, she's going to be fine. Your mom promised to come get us as soon as we can go back and see Haley."

He nodded, but didn't look quite sure. I couldn't blame him. In the last year, his entire world had been tilted off its axis.

"Want me to turn the channel to something you'd like?" I asked. There had to be cartoons or something more kid friendly than the morning news.

"Nah. Come on, Bitty. Let's see what's in your to-go bag."

Bitty was on my lap and I turned her so she was facing Jeremy, who started to dig in her bag.

"To-go bag?" came a voice.

I saw the man who was seated across from our chairs in the waiting room watching the kids.

"Jeremy's mom introduced me to the idea. She keeps a special backpack for each of the kids in the closet. She fills it with all kinds of surprises. Books and magazines. Coloring books and crayons. Small card games. They only get to open it up on outings that will take more than an hour. I figured a trip to the emergency room would certainly qualify. I suspect that we'll be here for more than that."

Heck we'd already been here longer than that.

Alice had put together Bitty's bag and hung it with the other kids'. She treated my daughter as if she was one of her own. Most of the time I simply counted myself lucky that she did, but sometimes I still felt a stab of guilt. I knew that I'd never set out to date a married man, but I had.

And always, on the heels of those thoughts came one more … I was my father's daughter.

I looked at Alice's son as he reached into Bitty's to-go bag and pulled out a construction paper book and said, "Mom didn't get this one. I made it for you and she put some stuff on it so you can't eat it."

He opened the first page. "Here's a picture of your mom." He flipped the page. "And your Aunt Alice." He flipped again. "And here's me and Haley."

He chewed on his lips and I recognized his anxiousness.

"She's fine," I reassured him.

Jeremy nodded and went back to looking at the pictures with Bitty.

"Haley is your daughter?" the stranger asked.

I looked at him. Really looked. He was nondescript. Brown hair cut so short you couldn't say it was a style. Brown eyes. He was tanner than most people in Erie, Pennsylvania were in the fall. His skin tone suggested he worked at some outdoor job.

He had a nice smile.

Maybe once upon a time, I'd have been attracted to him. I never liked men who were too smooth or too polished. He had on an Erie Otter's t-shirt and a pair of well-worn jeans. Yes, he looked comfortable and easy going. If I had a type, this was it.

But I didn't have a type anymore. There was no room in my life for a man right now.

"No, Charity's mine," I said, pointing to Bitty who was smacking the book as Jeremy valiantly kept trying to read it. "Jeremy and Haley are …"

I trotted out my new definition with no addition explanation. "They're family."

Alan was a creep and I might still be disgusted by his actions, but he'd given me such a gift in not only Bitty, but also Alice and the kids.

Alan had given me my family.

I still thought he was a creep, but it was easier to be civil to him when I remembered that.

"I'm Mark," the man I might have been attracted to under other circumstances, or at another time, said.

"And I'm not interested," I said nicely.

Not interested didn't go nearly far enough to describe how absolutely not looking for a new man I was.

"I wasn't hitting on you," he said with a grin and a small laugh.

I felt myself blushing. "I'm sorry, I mean..." There was no rescuing myself from that one, so I simply said, "I'm Olivia."

"How old is Haley?" he asked.

"Eight," I said. She'd been so stoic. So brave. I felt myself start to tear up, which I knew would worry Jeremy all the more, so I pushed the tears back and concentrated on the man who *wasn't* hitting on me. "Who are you waiting for?"

"My father. We spend a lot of time here," he said. I could hear the weariness that was woven into the words.

"I'm sorry," I said simply.

"Me, too."

Before either of us could say anything else, Mark's cellphone rang. He gave me a nod and picked it up. "Hello?"

There's no way not to listen to someone's conversation when they're sitting inches away from you. I caught enough of the Mark's side of the conversation to know he was talking about a tractor.

He hung up and turned around. "Sorry. Normally I wouldn't let a phone interrupt me, but I'm waiting for a delivery and I left them a message that I wouldn't be home when they came. I needed to touch base."

"Sorry. I know what it's like to juggle. I'm on a deadline and need to be working today, but..." I left the sentence hanging there lamely. I refused to think about the two chapters I had to finish translating this week. I'll confess, this book was taking me forever. I think it was so hard to work on because I didn't enjoy reading blood-and-gut books, but more than that, I knew I simply didn't like the protagonist.

Each page I translated felt like a slow drip water torture.

"What—" he started to ask.

But at that moment, Alice came into the waiting room.

"She's fine," she said. "They've got her hooked up to an IV for fluids and meds. She hasn't thrown up in the last hour, so I think we're over the worst of it."

"That's good," Jeremy said. "You should have heard her last night, Mom."

He did his best impression of Haley throwing up, and I'll confess, it was a good one.

"If I'd known she was sick..." Alice started.

"She didn't start throwing up until five, and I figured you'd be home in a few hours, but when she wouldn't stop...well, I thought bringing her here was the best option."

She nodded. "Thank you."

I'd forgotten about Mark. "Alice?" he said.

"Mark," Alice said. She gave him a hug. "Is it your dad?"

He nodded. "He'll never change."

I looked back and forth between them.

"We're friends," Alice said.

Mark added, "In addition to my father's frequent visits, I volunteer at the chapel here a few nights a week." Alice worked nights, which explained how they knew each other.

But I wasn't sure how someone *volunteered* at a chapel. It seemed to me there was more to it than that, but I simply nodded.

I turned back to Alice. She was looking back and forth between Mark and me. "Do you want me to take Jeremy home and—"

"No. I'm not goin' home. I gotta see Haley," Jeremy said.

Alice smiled. "Come on. Why don't you come check on her, then Olivia can take you and Bitty home."

"Maybe we'll make some soup," I said. "I bet Haley won't be up to eating anything heavier than that."

"Yeah, but if you're cookin' it, you gotta do a good job," Jeremy said.

"It's hard to burn soup," I pointed out.

Alice gave me a weary smile and said, "But if anyone could do it, it would be you."

Jeremy and Alice both laughed. I'd have liked to argue the point, but they were right, so I joined in.

"It was nice talking to you," I said to Mark, still chuckling. I picked up Bitty and the to-go bags and a diaper bag.

"You, too," he said.

We all made our way to the door and I glanced behind us at Mark. He was still standing there watching us leave. He nodded when he saw me look and I nodded back.

Part of me, wanted to go back and wait with him for news about his father.

No one should have to wait alone in the hospital. But I had the kids, and frankly, I didn't know him. I had all I could do to take care of the people I knew and loved. I didn't need to pick up anyone else's trouble.

Haley was sleeping when we got to her room.

"The medication will make her drowsy," Alice explained.

I nodded and looked down at the little girl who reminded me of her mother. Jeremy was the spitting image of Alan. I wondered if Bitty would look more like me or Alan as she got older.

Right after everything happened, I'd have said I hoped she looked like me because I didn't want daily reminders of him. But now when I saw shades of Alan in Bitty, I thought more of Jeremy than Alan.

Alice had said something once about her life not turning out as she'd planned, but she thought she was happier now than she'd every been.

I echoed her sentiment. This wasn't the life I'd planned, but it was a good one.

Haley opened her eyes. "Hey barfy," Jeremy said then imitated her again.

"Enough," Alice said.

Haley smiled. "It's okay."

Her eyes closed again. "Let's go home and start on that soup," I said to Jeremy.

"Don't worry, Hale. I'll keep an eye on Aunt Olivia so she don't burn it."

"Yeah, that's good. Burned soup would make me barf," she said sagely.

Alice smiled at the kids' teasing. "I'll probably be a few hours. They want to be sure she's done throwing up before they send us home."

"I can take Jeremy to school if you want?"

"No. I'm gonna wait for Haley to come home."

I looked at Alice, waiting for her decision.

"After such a busy night, I think staying home makes sense," she said. "I wouldn't want you to fall asleep at school."

We both could see the relief on his face as he said, "Thanks, Mom."

"So we'll be at home waiting for you," I said.

"Did you call Alan?" she asked.

I shook my head. "I didn't. I'm so sorry. I just didn't think..."

She held up her hand, stopping me. "Neither did I until just now. You and I have become so much a team that I don't tend to think about him, or worry about him. I should, but..." She glanced at Jeremy and just let the sentence end there.

I knew what she meant. Alan did come by on occasion. He still took the kids overnight for Alice now and then. But he wasn't a very present figure in our day-to-day lives.

When Alice had invited me into her home and confronted Alan with me, I knew she was a class act.

When she came to the hospital with me when I had Bitty, and stayed, I knew she was all heart.

And when she showed up the next day and drove me and the baby home... well, I knew she was one in a million.

She came over the next week or so and brought meals and gifts for Bitty.

By the time she told me she was selling her house with Alan and getting something smaller that she could afford on a single paycheck, I wasn't at all surprised by her strength. But when she asked me about sharing a house... well, I guess I wasn't surprised, but I was still amazed.

The duplex was perfect. We were close, without being on top of each other. I watched her kids when she worked nights, she took Bitty off my hands on her days off, and afternoons on days she slept. It made working easier.

I had other options. I could choose not to work, but as time went on, I found myself weighing my actions against what Alice would do. She'd become the big sister I'd never had. And I knew that Alice would never be content to sponge off her family.

I guess that was the measure of a good friend... someone who made you want to be better than your natural tendencies.

She smiled now. "I'll call Alan now. And you be good and help Olivia," she said to Jeremy.

"Sure. I gotta help her cook the soup. And I'll make Haley a bed on the couch like you make for me. And I'll bring down a bucket in case she pukes again so she don't make a mess and—"

"That all sounds good. Hopefully we'll be home around lunch time."

I took the kids home and the rest of the day was a blur, tending to Bitty and Jeremy and then helping where I could with Haley.

After Bitty went to bed, I went to work and finished another chapter of the book I didn't want to translate.

I didn't go to bed myself until two a.m.

And it wasn't until I was almost asleep that I thought about Mark and wondered how his father was.

Alice knew him. Maybe she'd know.

I promised myself I'd ask her the next day.

Chapter Eleven

Alice

On the plus side: I might not be the best mom, but at least I try.

Haley was fine. I knew that, but I couldn't help but feel guilty. If I hadn't stayed for coffee with Callum, I would have been home sooner. And if I'd been home...

I couldn't think of anything I'd have done differently.

Nothing would have changed.

Rationally, I knew that I couldn't be with my kids 24/7. And I knew that when we weren't together, things could happen. Maybe every mother's job was finding a compromise between helicopter-parenting and being unconcerned.

It felt like a tightrope and I swayed back and forth between both options as I tried to wend my way through the kids' childhood.

Still as I tucked the kids in that night, I spent a few extra minutes, wishing I could bundle them up in bubble-wrap and keep them safe from everything. I wanted to protect them from every heartache, every bad choice, every illness or injury.

I knew I couldn't.

People talk about the downsides of parenting. The terrible twos. The snotty prepubescent years. The awful teens.

But I knew that the worst part of parenting was the moment you realized that you couldn't keep your kids safe, no matter how hard you tried.

I went downstairs to the living room with a very quiet phone in my back pocket.

Olivia tapped on the door that separated her place from mine. "Come in," I called.

She walked in with Bitty on her hip. Bitty held out her arms when she saw me.

I picked her up and nuzzled her neck, which made her laugh. And then realized that no matter how hard Olivia and I tried, we couldn't keep her safe either.

I was depressing the heck out of myself.

I grasped at straws and finally managed to find a plus side. *On the plus side: all three kids were safe and healthy right now.* Well, Haley was on her way back to being healthy. She hadn't thrown up again since we left the hospital.

The thought settled me and I nuzzled Bitty again for good measure. Her laughter was a balm.

"So are you going to tell me about it?" Olivia asked without preamble.

I took Bitty to the couch and she snuggled close. It was almost her bedtime and she had that limp feeling to her muscles. I knew it wouldn't be long before she'd conked out.

"And don't tell me nothing's wrong," Olivia warned as she sat down next to us. "Also don't try to blame it on worry for Haley, though I know you worry about the kids. We both do. This is something else. And I suspect the *something* is that man you were having coffee with. He's the reason you've been home a few minutes later on work days?"

I nodded.

"And all the text messages?" she asked.

"Yes. But other than one text checking on Haley, my phone's been decidedly quiet."

We'd had slow-text evenings before because we both had real lives that pulled us away from the phone, but this was too quiet.

Deep down I knew that he wasn't going to be calling or texting again anytime soon. I'd known it the moment I saw his expression when Olivia and the kids came in.

"Uncharacteristically quiet?" she asked softly.

I nodded.

"Then he's a booger-eating butt-head," she said angrily.

"Jeremy?" I asked.

I was smiling despite myself, which I knew had been her intent. My son had become very inventive with his name-calling. He toed the line and avoided the words I'd absolutely vetoed, but he came up with unique ways to use the words he was allowed.

"Yes," Olivia said. "We had a long talk about name calling, but you have to admit, it's an inventive name."

I smiled. Having Alan leave had been hard on Jeremy. I never said a word against his father, but the kids knew he hadn't been around much for them. They vacillated between emotions quicker than a pendulum.

"The man in question was..." I wasn't sure how to explain what he'd been to me. "He was uncomplicated. We didn't exchange anything more than first names and then spent a few weeks talking about books and television. I'm not ready for anything more than that, and frankly, even if I were, I wouldn't have time for anything more than that."

"But..." Olivia started.

I wrapped my arms a little tighter around Bitty, drinking in the scent of freshly bathed baby.

"There are no buts about it. The two of us worked while we stayed in our little bubble of anonymity. Then the real world intruded and the bubble burst. I don't think we're going to work without that..."

"Bubble?" Olivia supplied.

I nodded. Before she could offer up another argument, I added, "And I don't think you can try to argue me out of it because I've noticed you haven't asked me to keep Bitty while you go out on a hot date."

Olivia laughed. "What can I say, I'm in love... with a baby. And I'm fortunate to have you for a friend. You understand in a way no one else could."

That was true.

Olivia nodded slightly, as if she'd asked herself a question and was answering herself. "You know that guy in the waiting room that you knew?" She hesitated a moment, as if looking for his name. "Mark?"

I nodded.

"His dad was there. Could you check next time you're at work how he is?"

"The dad or Mark?" I asked.

"His dad, of course," Olivia said.

I wasn't buying it. She was interested. And if I was right, he hadn't seemed immune to her either.

Olivia was younger than I was. Enough younger that she should be out meeting new people. And while Mark and I weren't bosom friends, I knew him well enough to know that he was a nice guy.

Mark was everything that Alan had proven himself not to be.

I didn't say any of that. And I didn't tease Olivia. I just nodded and said, "Sure. I'll ask around."

Mark and Olivia?

I'd have to think about getting the two of them together in a nonchalant way.

Thinking about Olivia and Mark was easier than thinking about Callum and the fact he hadn't texted me.

Not that I'd texted him either.

The next morning, I got up and made the coffee with no friendly *bing* on my phone telling me I had a text.

That was fine.

I mean, how much could I miss someone I'd only known a handful of weeks? I didn't even know his last name.

Getting over Callum would be easy.

Chapter Twelve

Alice

On the plus side: Routine is another way of saying rut.
Sometimes it's good to shake things up.

$\mathcal{I}$woke up with a start. Jeremy was standing next to my bed staring at me, just like he used to do when he was little. He used to *stare me awake* on a regular basis.

When I was little, I had a cat that could do that. She'd stare me awake when she was ready for breakfast, regardless of what time it was.

"What's wrong?" I asked, trying to glance around him at the clock.

He wasn't see-through, so I had no idea what time it was.

"Haley's barfing again," he said.

I sprang out of bed and almost stepped in Haley's vomit. There was a trail between her room and the bathroom. She'd obviously tried to make it and hadn't succeeded.

I spent the next twenty minutes holding her hair back as she puked and placing cold washcloths on the back of her neck or on her forehead.

When she was done, I tucked her back in, then spent the next twenty minutes cleaning up vomit from the carpet.

I did my best, then used a foam carpet cleaner, thinking that would make it smell better.

It only succeeded in adding a lovely floral undercurrent to the vomit smell.

I took a shower before I went back to bed, only to discover that Haley was sick again.

This time she made it to the bathroom.

It was five o'clock before I went back to bed for good, and it was seven when I got up with Jeremy. I called Alan and asked him to pick Jeremy up for school. He began to hem and haw, but then I said fine, he could stay with the vomit princess.

Alan drove Jeremy to school.

I tried to decide if I needed to take Haley back in to the doctor's. You'd think being a nurse would make decisions like that clear-cut. I was pretty sure it was just a bug, but as a nurse I also knew that her nausea could be a sign of so many other things.

Food poisoning.

Infections.

Brain and central nervous system issues.

Some kind of systemic disease or infection.

I checked in on her, but she was still sleeping. I wasn't going to wake her to take her in somewhere.

Haley woke up a bit before lunch and said she was hungry.

I kept her on clear liquids and made her a bed on the couch. We spent the rest of the day snuggling.

I couldn't keep her safe from everything and I knew it. But today I could hold her and snuggle next to her on the couch. I could watch Disney princess movies with her.

That was enough.

As long as I was up, we invited Bitty over so Olivia could get some work done in peace and quiet.

Neither of us worried about Bitty catching whatever Haley had. They were so close that she'd already been exposed.

I went to go get both girls a drink and came back to see Bitty snuggled up next to Haley on the couch.

They were both singing along with Belle.

Haley's hair was long, wavy and was somewhere between brown and blonde.

Bitty's hair was white-blonde and hung in wild ringlets.

Despite the differences, it was easy to see they were sisters.

I melted as I watched them. I joined them on the couch and started signing with them.

Bitty fell asleep along with Haley after lunch. They were still snuggling.

I got out my phone and took a bunch of pictures, then texted one to Olivia next door with the caption ... *shhh*.

I grabbed a nap with them.

I was humming *Let It Go* when I showed up for work that night. Haley hadn't thrown up again all day, so I was pretty sure that Olivia was safe.

The shift went quickly.

When it was over, I went down to the gym, took a shower, and walked to the coffee stand.

I stood near a corner and watched as people began to line up.

Callum wasn't one of them.

Not that I expected him to be.

Still, I'd hoped.

I found I didn't have any inclination to get coffee on my own, so I turned around to leave and practically bumped into Darren Marker. He was a nice x-ray technician I'd met a few times.

The hospital was big enough that I *didn't* know more people than I *did* know. And I knew more people on a nod-and-smile basis than people I knew by name.

"Sorry, Darren," I apologized.

"No problem. Hey, I was thinking about you the other day" he said.

"Oh? A problem with one of my patients?" I couldn't think of who it could be or what could have happened.

He shook his head. "I was wondering if you'd like to go out sometime."

I didn't know what to do... what to say. I'd been married a long time and I wasn't looking to get back into dating circles.

I thought about Callum and realized I'd been thinking about dating him.

If I were being honest, I was ready to say *yes* to a date right before Olivia and the kids came in.

"Darren, it's sweet of you to ask, but I don't think I'm ready to date anyone just yet." It was a lie, but a hopefully a kind one.

"What if we just got coffee?" he asked.

I felt tears well up in my eyes.

"I don't think that would be wise," I said, my voice breaking as I spoke.

"I'm sorry, Alice," he said with that look of horror on his face all men wore when they faced a crying female.

"No, I'm sorry. It's been a long couple days. I'm truly flattered," I managed before I beat a hasty retreat down the hall.

Not having Callum around shouldn't be hard to adjust to. I had only known him a couple months.

But I knew it would be difficult. I'd allowed him to become a part of the fabric of my crazy life.

That had been my mistake.

Chapter Thirteen

Olivia

*On the plus side: There's no need to be a good cook if you have
a best friend who enjoys cooking.*

Alice had been in a funk for weeks. I knew it had to do
with her mystery texter who was no longer texting.

And I'd noticed on mornings she worked, she was home
earlier than normal. I wondered if this had to do with him as
well. She didn't seem inclined to talk about him and I wasn't
inclined to push.

But on Thanksgiving morning, she was downright bubbly
as we prepared dinner.

I was roasting the turkey and making the potatoes.

I was not the world's best cook, but I was determined to get
this right. Mashing the potatoes was well within my skill set,
but the turkey made me nervous. I read everything I could find
on various methods. You would think that there would be one
universal way to make a foolproof turkey, but oh no. There were
a bunch.

I watched an Alton Brown show on brining turkeys. He
swore I would love it and I trusted Alton. Really, there weren't

many men I trusted anymore, but Alton seemed so confident in my abilities that I was allowing myself to trust in him.

So the day before the big day, I stuck that bird into a giant container of brine that I'd flavored with spices and a bottle of wine. Every time I opened the fridge, I stared at the pot, hoping the turkey was doing its part.

I kept telling myself that I could handle the turkey and potatoes, trying to believe in my abilities as much as Alton did.

Alice was cooking everything else. It was a wise decision on both our parts.

I got up early on Thanksgiving morning and took my turkey out of the brine. I patted it dry and put it in my brand new roasting pan.

After Bitty was up, I checked in at Alice's. We set up the dinner in her dining room, which was probably a good thing. My *office* was my dining room table and it looked like a tornado hit it. I was a piler. Papers relating to books and dictionaries and thesauruses were piled everywhere.

I could have used online dictionaries and thesauruses, but there was something about the tactile nature of dealing with the real resource book that worked for me.

Half the time, I'd figured out what word I needed while I looked it up.

My brain just needed that quiet time to work it out for itself.

Alice, being Alice, had everything in hand at her place, so I went back to mine and started peeling potatoes.

Bitty was siting in her new high chair. It was one of the plastic ones that was designed to be hooked onto a regular chair. I set it on my huge kitchen island as I peeled potatoes. It was a big island, so I was sure she wasn't going to topple off. She was pretty much eye level with me.

Not that she was looking at me.

She was busy chasing a piece yogurt bites—her not-so-secret addiction—as she babbled and drooled so copiously I was afraid the yogurt bite was going to melt on the tray before she could manage to pick it up.

I laughed at her antics, which made her laugh as well.

Bitty never quite knew why someone was laughing, but she was always happy to join in.

My phone rang, interrupting the moment.

It was a FaceTime call.

And I groaned as I saw the name on the screen.

I wiped my hand on a towel and swiped the button over, opening the app.

"Happy Thanksgiving, Mother," I said, forcing a smile.

My mother's picture came into focus. Every hair was in place and she was wearing her grandmother's pearls.

"You look lovely," I added.

"Happy Thanksgiving. I'm sure you'll look lovely, too, once you've changed for dinner."

I did not mention that my turtleneck sweater was as dressed as I was going to get.

And I certainly didn't mention that I had on jeans, not *slacks*.

"Don't forget a bit of blush when you do," she added. "You look pale."

"Thanks," I said, reining in the sarcasm.

I turned the camera so she could see Bitty. "Say hello to Grandma, Bitty."

"Are you still calling the child by that horrid nickname?" my mother asked.

"The kids gave it to her and I think it fits," I said calmly. It wasn't a lie, just fudging the facts. Alice gave her the name and the kids embraced it.

No apologies. No excuses.

Instead, I asked, "So when do your guests arrive?"

"Not until five or so," she said. "Dinner will be served at seven. How about you?"

I knew she was trying to make conversation. Trying to find neutral ground was always an issue for us. "We're eating early because the kids are going to Alan's this evening for a second Thanksgiving. His mother's back in town."

"How you can let him—"

I stopped her, knowing that this particular conversation route would lead us no place good. "He's making an effort. And he is Bitty's father."

"And that woman?" my mother asked.

That-woman was my mother's name for Alice, as if somehow Alice was the other-woman, not me.

"That's who I'm having dinner with," I said softly.

Ready to cut my losses, I hurriedly added, "And these potatoes aren't going to peel themselves, so I'd better run. I need to pull the turkey out in precisely forty-nine minutes so it can rest before we eat. Send my love to everyone."

I didn't ask about my father or name him specifically because I generally avoided mentioning him if I could help it.

"I will. Have a good day, Olivia. And don't forget the blush."

I hung up. "I love you, too, Mom," I said to the blank screen.

"And that Bitty, was your grandmother. She's a tough old bird, but she cares about us in her own way."

I tried to remind myself of that fact often.

My mother wasn't the type of mother I'd longed for when I was growing up, but she was who she was. I could either accept that, or beat my head against the wall wishing things were different.

I worked at simply accepting her.

She did not always return the favor.

To be honest, she *never* returned the favor.

I went back to peeling and occasionally put another yogurt bite on Bitty's tray. I tried to keep reminding myself that my mother did care. I told myself that the reason she'd never come to Erie to meet Bitty was because she was getting older and travel was hard. Of course, she told me all about her trip to Paris with my cousin Hilary.

Hilary was more a sister than cousin. She was also the daughter my mother wished she'd had.

"Do you need any help?" Alice called as she walked through the open door, through the living room, and into the kitchen. "I have the table set and I don't have the next wave of work in my kitchen for a half hour."

"I'm almost done with the potatoes and the turkey looks fine. I just pulled the foil off so it'll brown."

"It smells good," she said.

Alice gave Bitty another yogurt bite. "I wish they'd had these when Jeremy and Haley were little. She's a bit addicted."

"She is," I agreed, smiling at my daughter. "I make myself feel good about using them as entertainment by telling myself they're good for her fine motor skills as well as good for her nutritionally."

"Both are true. Plus they keep her quiet for a few minutes. I don't know if you've noticed, she is not a quiet child by nature. Neither are her siblings."

I laughed. "Maybe just a bit of it. Speaking of not-quiet-by-nature, where are the kids?"

"Making place cards for the table," she said.

"Oh, that's sweet. I would never have thought of that." And that's another reason why Hilary was the daughter my mother always wanted. Hilary would think about things like place cards and dressing for dinner.

"That's me. Suzie Homemaker," Alice said with a bit of a laugh. "At least I used to be. You should have seen my pantry back in the day. It was so neat and organized. Looking back, I'm pretty sure it was a sign of some mental impairment. Come over when you're done here."

I put the potatoes on the stove, picked up Bitty and walked over to see the kids' project. The table looked beautiful, but something didn't add up.

"Who—" I started to ask, but the doorbell rang and Alice took off towards it.

I walked around the table with Bitty on my hip. There was Alice's name. The kids' names. A small place card on Bitty's highchair tray. My name and...

I looked up as Alice and Mark walked into the room. Her smile was just a bit too bright. And her expression was totally too pleased with herself.

"Mark," I said, genuinely pleased to see him.

But for good measure, I turned and shot Alice a look of warning. She didn't look the least bit abashed.

"Olivia. I didn't know Alice invited you as well." He looked pleased, which was good.

"I live right through there," I said, pointing at the open door.

"Alice didn't mention you were neighbors," he said.

"I suspect there's a lot Alice didn't mention," I said. Just like she didn't mention to me that our family dinner would include a guest.

Mark looked back and forth between us. "Sorry she sprung me on you."

I wanted to be annoyed, but I couldn't quite manage it. "It's a pleasant surprise. I was just checking out the kids' place cards."

"They're nice," he said. "Everything looks nice and the smell is out of this world."

"Thanks," both Alice and I said together.

"Hey, Mr. Mark," Jeremy said as he ran into the dining room. "Mom said she asked you to come. She said you got cows and chickens and pigs on your farm and if I asked you, you'd tell me all about them."

Haley came in after him. "Hi," she said shyly.

"Oh yeah, that's Haley. She's the one who was barfing when we were at the hospital, so you didn't meet her."

"It's my pleasure to meet you now," Mark said. "I'm glad to see you're feeling better."

Haley smiled at him and Bitty realized she was being ignored. She held out her arms in the universal symbol that Mark was supposed to pick her up.

He obliged as if it were second nature and before I knew it, he was sitting with Bitty on his leg, coloring with the older kids as he talked about the farm.

I let them go and followed Alice into her kitchen. "Alice Collins, just what do you think you're doing?"

"Olivia Weiss, I'm sure I don't know what you're talking about." Her expression said she knew exactly what I was talking about. There was a devilish twinkle in her eye.

I had to admit to myself that she looked happier than she'd looked since the kids and I interrupted her morning coffee when Haley was sick.

Knowing that made it difficult to get too huffy about Mark's invitation, but I put some effort into being just huffy enough to dissuade her from future matchmaking attempts.

"Alice, Mark seems nice. Very nice. Watching him with the kids ... well, it's nice. But I'm not in the market for ..." I hesitated. "For anything. Or anyone. Nice or not."

"Olivia, that was a lot of *nice*. And you're young. You have your whole life in front of you."

I snorted. "I know you're a bit older than I am, but you're not exactly ancient."

"*A bit* is an understatement. I'm in my mid-thirties."

"Oooh, a decade. Wow." I snorted. And as I did, I realized my mother wouldn't approve of the noise, anymore than she'd approve of my still unblushed cheeks.

I ran next door to check on my portion of the dinner.

The turkey looked awesome, but I was still nervous as I recovered it with foil to let it rest.

The potatoes were whipped to perfection. And when I finally put the turkey on the platter, I snuck a bite from the underside.

"It's amazing," I proclaimed as I carried the bird to Alice's. "Yeah, I'm a cooking goddess, if I do say so myself."

Alice laughed. "Now, if only you could translate that new cooking power to macaroni and cheese," she teased.

Jeremy took the bait and proceeded to tell Mark how I'd put too much milk into the sauce. He proclaimed loudly that I had tried to feed him macaroni and cheese soup. "Then Olivia tried to pour the milk off and it was just plain noodles," Haley finished for her brother.

"And those weren't half bad with a bit of butter, salt and pepper," I said.

We all sat at our assigned seats and Alice asked Mark to say grace before we dug in.

As we ate dinner—and the marvelous turkey—I couldn't help but think that maybe Alice's extra decade gave her additional insight, because she was right. Mark was definitely worth knowing.

He listened to Jeremy and Haley with a focused attention that I'd noticed many adults were lacking when conversing with children.

He laughed when Bitty tried a bite of mashed potatoes and spit them out in his direction. They landed on his shirt and he calmly wiped them up as I apologized profusely.

He insisted on helping clear the dinner dishes and was beyond gracious when Alan showed up to get the kids.

And that, in and of itself, said a lot about him, because Alan was anything but gracious. He about twisted himself in two trying to decide whether Mark was at dinner because of Alice or me.

Yeah, I know I couldn't really read Alan's mind, but despite being a liar and a cheat, he was fairly easy to read. And his cold hostility towards Mark was almost palpable. And it was sooo hypocritical.

I kissed the baby and then shut the door as Alice walked out with him and the kids.

Alan glanced behind and shot eye-daggers in Mark's direction.

"So what was that?" Mark asked.

"Did Alice explain how we met?" I asked.

He shook his head.

We went into my living room and I told him the whole story. At one point, Alice looked in, realized what we were talking about and popped back out.

As I finished, I waited to see the judgment in his eyes.

I'd seen it in my parents' eyes when I'd first told them I was unmarried and pregnant.

I'd seen it again when I'd told them that Alan was out of the picture and why.

And I saw it a third time when I told them I was giving up my apartment near the university and moving into a duplex with Alice.

I understood where my mother was coming from, but when I saw that look of judgment in my father's eyes, I was incensed. He was the last man on earth who had the right to judge me.

I didn't tell Mark any of that, but telling him about Alan brought all those emotions to the surface.

I planned to tell him what to do with his opinion when I spotted it.

But as I wound down, judgment was not what I saw in Mark's eyes. I saw compassion and maybe something else.

"You two are amazing," he said softly.

"Pardon?" I asked. That was not what I'd thought I'd hear.

"You and Alice," he clarified. "You took this horrible moment and you turned it into something else entirely. You've become a family."

I didn't know what to say to that, but I was saved from trying to find something when Mark patted my hand and continued. "Everyone is looking for their family—for where they belong. You two found it. You don't know how lucky that is."

There was a wistful look in his eyes, and I realized he was speaking from experience.

"You're the first person to ever put it that way, but that's exactly how I feel. Lucky," I said.

I'd never said the words out loud, or even really articulated them in my head, but that was truly how I felt. *Lucky.*

And at that moment, Mark leaned forward slowly.

I knew he was going to kiss me. There was plenty of time for me to pull away, but I didn't. And when his lips gently touched mine, I realized how much I liked it.

Last time I jumped into a relationship without really knowing the other person, it was with Alan.

I wouldn't make that mistake again, so I pulled back, ending the kiss.

"Mark, we really don't know each other and I'm not looking to …" I hesitated and then found the words. "Rush in. I'm not looking to rush into anything. It's been eleven months and I've hardly caught my breath and …"

"Shh," he said. "It's okay. I know it might surprise you, given the circumstances, but I'm not one to rush a relationship. But I'd like to get to know you better. And maybe let you get to know me better and then see where that takes us."

I found myself nodding my head. "I'd like that."

"Maybe we could start with taking a walk?" he asked.

"That would be nice."

"And maybe, if you don't think I'm being too forward, you'd let me hold your hand?"

I laughed, not because what he said was funny really, but because the idea of walking with Mark and maybe holding his hand made me feel schoolgirl-bubbly inside, and the only thing I could do with those bubbles was let them escape in my laughter.

"Yes," I said. "We should invite Alice though."

"Of course. Slow courtships require a chaperone."

When we asked her, Alice just smiled and said she had plans.

I knew her plans didn't include her mystery texter and I felt bad about that.

"Are you sure?" I asked.

"Yes. You two run along." She shooed us as if we were Jeremy and Haley.

As we walked down the sidewalk, it started to snow. Mark reached out his gloved hand and held my mittened one.

And it was pretty much perfect.

Chapter Fourteen

Alice

On the Plus Side: Watching young love
rekindled something that felt as if it had gone cold in me.
It took a few moments to identify the feeling.
Hope.

I watched as mark and Olivia walked down the street together. As it started to snow and I smiled to myself. If I had a camera, I'd have captured the moment.

A moment when two young people were entering the world of *what-if.*

Maybe Olivia was right. Maybe they would eventually walk away from each other, deciding they didn't fit.

As I had the thought, they both reached out simultaneously and took the other's hand.

And I truly didn't believe that they would be walking away.

If nothing else, I suspected they'd be at least friends.

But as they turned the corner, still hand-in-hand, I believed there was a better chance they'd be something more.

I'm not sure why.

Playing matchmaker wasn't my forte.

Still, there was something about the two of them. I saw it as they sat in the waiting room with Jeremy and Bitty.

And I saw it today at dinner.

I was so happy for Olivia. She deserved so much. And obviously, Alan wasn't it.

I looked at my cellphone and wished it would give the happy little beep that I'd come to associate with Callum's texts.

But it was silent on the table.

Suddenly, I was mad. Furious even. How dare he...

How dare he what?

He was a nice man who shared a few morning coffees with me and discussed some books and shows. He didn't owe me anything.

I didn't owe him anything.

And just as quickly as it came, my anger faded.

I didn't understand what I'd had with Callum. It couldn't really even qualify as a friendship. Friends knew things about each other.

And while I felt I knew things about Callum, they were ethereal, flimsy things.

The moment the real world intruded, they'd burst.

I thought I'd healed from Alan. If not healed, I was definitely *healing*.

I was going to have to face the fact that Callum had been one of those people who came into my life and then left without explanation.

And I was pretty sure, he was leaving me a better person. Not because of anything big he'd done or we'd done together. But maybe because he reminded me that not all men were like Alan.

Of course, I knew that. I'd seen enough relationships at work. But Callum had forced me to remember that I knew it at a point in my life when I'd needed the nudge.

I couldn't be bitter about that.

I couldn't even mourn losing Callum.

I would simply look back at those mornings with him with fondness.

He might not need to say goodbye but I did, I realized.

I went over and picked my phone up from the table that was covered with Jeremy's Lego people and one of Haley's Barbies.

I texted Callum: *Happy Thanksgiving.*

I knew as I typed it I was saying goodbye.

I put down my phone, not expecting a reply.

And that was okay.

I was thankful for the time we'd had together.

The house was quiet.

There were plenty of leftovers for dinner.

I went and picked up a Harry Dresden book, curled up on the couch and read it, even though I knew I'd never discuss it with Callum.

Chapter Fifteen

Alice

On the plus side: Immediately after a child is born, you measure time in small increments. They're an hour old. A day old. A week old. Finally they're a year old. After that you start to measure time in broader strokes. It's like that with life, too.

There are a few things more awkward than getting together with the man you've recently divorced. But getting together with him on the one-year anniversary of the day you kicked him out definitely made things more awkward.

Bitty's first birthday party was on Sunday. We invited Alan.

Olivia's cousin, Hilary, who I'd never met, came into town for the event. Olivia had invited her to stay at the house ... she'd declined. She said she'd made arrangements and would simply join us for the party.

So it was just Olivia and I getting ready for Bitty's party while Jeremy and Haley *babysat* in the middle of Olivia's living room floor.

Olivia had taken Jeremy and Haley shopping for party decorations and they'd decided that Bitty wanted a *Star Wars* themed party.

I might have doubted the validity of that statement, but Olivia was a pushover and agreed that Star Wars was *obviously* just the thing for a first birthday.

We hung the Death Star from the chandelier over her table. Olivia had an eclectic, do-it-herself style. The table was an old oak one that she'd picked up at a house sale. She'd used a router (a tool I'd never heard of until she got it out her tool pile in the basement) and then painted the whole thing black and laid slate tiles in the sunken center.

I would never have thought of doing something like that, but it ended up being beautiful. Most of the time I didn't notice it because it was covered with papers, books, and her laptop. Today I noticed.

Olivia had taken to going to house-sales this winter and a lot of her pieces were secondhand remakes.

She said it was the ultimate green endeavor. She was saving the planet by upcycling her décor.

"Be careful," I said as she tottered on the table.

"How's that?" she asked.

"It looks good...well, as good as a star of death can look."

She laughed.

"I can't believe that you okayed *Star Wars* for Bitty's first birthday party," I said. "You indulge my kids more than I do."

She laughed. "They're good kids and they'll remember the party more than Bitty ever will." She paused and added, "And just wait until you see the party hats. I knitted them."

Olivia was a renaissance woman of the first order. "You knitted *Star Wars* hats?"

She nodded. "Just some. Princess Leia for Bitty. A Yoda hat for Jeremy. Haley has R2D2 and you're Queen Amidala."

"And you?" I asked.

"C3PO. I asked Hilary if she wanted a party hat. She said no." Olivia frowned. "I should warn you, she can be a bit difficult. And I'm being generous when I say *a bit.*"

I patted her shoulder. "I think you and I can handle difficult. Speaking of which, what's Alan's hat?"

Her momentary pain gave wait to mirth. "Darth."

I burst out laughing.

"What's so funny?" Jeremy called.

"What do you call a pirate droid?" I called back, purposefully saying *droid.*

Olivia gave me a smile of acknowledgement.

"I dunno," Jeremy said.

I drew out the "Arrrrgh," then with just the right umph added, "2D2."

Olivia and Haley laughed, but Jeremy just rolled his eyes.

Olivia passed out the hats and I stuck mine on my head. "It fits nicely. Really, Darth?" I asked quietly, chuckling softly.

"Hey, I figure you and I have been wonderful about everything. We really are fantastic, generous ladies," she said with a grin. "Awesome even. I won't talk badly about him to the kids, but seriously, he sort of does embody certain qualities that make that hat the perfect option."

I was still laughing when there was a knock on Olivia's door.

"I'll get it," I said.

I was wearing good jeans, a grey t-shirt and a black cardigan and felt like I had managed to be put together. I opened the door with my Princess hat on—the capper on my party outfit. Literally.

The woman standing on Olivia's doorstep was wearing a super fancy outfit. I'm sure this particular woolish looking combo had some designer's name attached to it.

She frowned when she saw me, but I forced a smile. "You must be Hilary. I'm Olivia's friend, Alice. Come in." She stepped inside and I shut the door. "We're so glad you could make it to Bitty's party."

"Bitty?" she asked.

"Charity's nickname," I said.

She rolled her eyes and I wasn't sure if it was that nicknames were bad form or this particular nickname was simply bad. I ignored her expression and offered, "Can I take your coat?"

"You *may*," she said, heavy emphasis on the *may*.

Suddenly I was a kid again and my mother was lecturing me on grammar. My mom didn't have a lot of room to lecture about many things, but grammar was her bailiwick and she made sure to let me know it whenever the opportunity presented itself.

"Please come in," I said.

I led her to Olivia and quickly made my escape, leaving Olivia to deal with her cousin.

"Mom, Bitty's trying to eat a piece of paper," Haley called.

I hurried over to the baby, who was indeed munching on paper.

"Ick," Jeremy said. "I tried to get it out of her mouth, but she bit me."

"Guess that's why we call her *Bitty*," Haley said, and started laughing at her own joke.

I managed to get the paper out of the baby's mouth with all my fingers intact.

Haley and Jeremy took off to Olivia's, probably to share their joke.

I picked up Bitty, ready to go join them all, when the doorbell rang again.

This time it was my door rather than Olivia's.

Alan. I sighed.

Of course, he knew that our living rooms connected, but it still seemed as if he should have knocked on Olivia's door. It was her party for their daughter, after all.

I opened the door.

"Alice..." Alan said. That was it. He ran out of things to say.

Which was fine, because really, we didn't have anything to talk about if we weren't talking about the kids.

I was saved from having to think of something to fill the dead air because Haley and Jeremy had followed me over and screeched when the spotted him. "Daddy."

Haley launched herself at him and Alan caught her. Jeremy grabbed his hand and said, "Come on. You gotta see the decorations. And you gotta get your birthday hat. Bitty loves *Star Wars*, don't you Bitty."

The baby babbled her response.

"Guess why we call Bitty Bitty?" Jeremy said.

"Why?" Alan asked.

"Let me tell him," Haley cried.

As the kids argued about who would deliver the punch line, they dragged Alan into Olivia's.

He admired the decorations as he managed to take off his coat. Olivia's doorbell rang.

"I'll get it," I shouted and left Alan to deal with the three kids.

This time, my smile of welcome was genuine when I saw it was Mark.

"Hi," I said, happy to see him. That there was only one out of three guests who I would enjoy spending an afternoon with didn't speak of very good odds. "Come on in."

He had a huge package in his hands and I realized that Alan hadn't brought anything with him. I remembered him telling me that Jeremy didn't need any gifts for his first birthday and Christmas because he was too young to remember him.

I'd overridden him, but left to his own devices, he'd chosen to ignore a gift.

Which made me like Mark even more.

"Need help?" I asked.

He shook his head. "Nah. It's bulky, but not too heavy." He kicked off his boots, which I realized Alan hadn't done either.

I reminded myself sternly that not only wouldn't I allow myself to compare Alan to other men. I would try not to judge him. He was who he was. Last year at this time, all the things he *was* mattered to me, but now, the only thing that really concerned me was that he was the kids' father. I would be patient and as kind as I could, if only for that reason.

Feeling better after my brief mental scolding, I led Mark into Olivia's. He sat the present down. He barely got his coat off before the kids ambushed him. "Mark," they screamed.

"Rugrats," he countered.

"Mark, this is Alan. Alan, Mark."

"How do you know my family?" Alan asked, as if he didn't remember Mark from Thanksgiving.

It was a challenge.

One I wasn't going to put up with. "He's a friend," I said simply as Olivia and Hilary came out of the kitchen with a wookie cake.

When Olivia spotted Mark, she lit up. I glanced at him and wasn't surprised to see that so did he.

"Hi," she said.

"Hi," he said.

Alan and Hilary both gave him chilly nods. Then Hilary looked at Alan.

I'd thought that Hilary had been cold to me and Mark, but her glacial reaction to Alan made me feel better about her.

"Olivia, the cake is amazing," I said.

She grinned. "Thanks. I ordered it."

"That means it'll taste good," Jeremy said.

"Hey, my turkey at Christmas was good, just like at Thanksgiving." I knew that Olivia took pride in that one dish she'd perfected.

"Yeah, but that cake's not turkey, is it?" Jeremy teased.

We all laughed, including Olivia.

Well, all except Alan who was too busy glaring at Mark, and Hilary who was too busy glaring at Alan.

"I think Olivia has a party-hat for you," I said to Mark.

I handed him the brown cowlish hat.

He cocked his head, asking me for help identifying the character.

"Obi Wan," I whispered.

I didn't say so, but I knew that the hat was for the Ewan McGregor Obi. Olivia confessed that she had a slight crush on both the actor and the character.

I looked at *Darth* Alan and smiled as *Obi* Mark slipped the hat on.

Yeah, I might not set up people very often, but this once, I'd done an extremely good job of it.

We all sang *happy birthday* and then Olivia put the baby in her highchair. The kids had picked out the wookie cake for Bitty and she went to town. Soon brown and blue icing stained her cheeks and her fingers were literally caked in cake.

"I don't know how much cake she actually managed to eat," Olivia said.

"Well, look at it this way, better a bath in the afternoon than a baby on a sugar high," I responded as the kids whooped for their sister, who then cheered for herself.

Alan and Hilary remained painfully silent as the rest of us chattered.

Mark pretended not to notice that the two of them were borderline rude. The kids were all oblivious.

Haley and Jeremy dug into their cake. I snapped pictures. The kids chortled as Bitty continued to play with the crumpled mass that had been her cake.

I took a load of dishes to the kitchen and as I came in I noticed Alan and Hilary sitting silently in the chairs. They didn't smile and certainly didn't engage with the kids. Maybe Olivia and I were simply used to the chaos. I watched as she finally took off Bitty's highchair tray, scooped her up and wiped up the worst of the frosting while she laughed at something Haley said.

Neither of our guests offered to help, so I called, "What can I do?"

Olivia smiled. "Entertain our guests while I give Bits here a quick dunk? After she's a bit cleaner, we can open presents."

"Sure," I said, wishing she'd offered to let me give Bitty a quick bath ... or a long one.

Mark, without asking, started gathering dishes. I'd like nothing more than to help him, but I felt I had to play hostess for Olivia.

"Can I get anyone anything else?" I asked.

"I'd like more cake," Jeremy tried.

I laughed and shook my head. "Good try."

He laughed as well. "Come on, Haley. We'll go help Olivia with Bitty. You know she likes to splash us."

The kids ran upstairs before I had a chance to stop them. Things went from awkward to more awkward as we all listened to the thud of their feet on the stairs.

Hilary pulled out her phone, glanced at it and said, "If you'll pardon me. I have to make a call."

That left me and my ex-husband. I did not feel the need to entertain him, so I started clearing off the rest of the table.

Alan followed me and grabbed at my hand. "I want to talk to you about child support—" he started.

I pulled my hand back from his as Jeremy ran back down the stairs. "Hey, Mom."

I cut Alan off. "Not now."

"You don't understand. Between you and Olivia I'm—"

Jeremy looked at us and I saw his concern.

"Darth this is not the time nor is it the place to discuss turning me to the dark side." I nodded at our son. "What's up, sweetheart?"

"I wanted to know if Dad would come see my wind turbine for the science fair."

Jeremy had worked on it for weeks. I was not much help. Occasionally I could order a part he needed, and once he let me hand him screwdrivers, but otherwise, I didn't understand how it worked, but Jeremy seemed confident it would.

It's an amazing moment when you realize that your child knows more about a subject than you did ... or ever would.

Alan for once didn't let me down. "Sure," he said. Jeremy started toward the stairs and Alan said to me, "Fine. I'll call you. I just need you and Olivia to know, I can't keep up these payments," to me.

Part of me wanted to be a nice guy and say, *fine. I'll manage.*

If we were talking about money for myself, I would. Pride would win out. But because the money was for the kids, I wouldn't. Not because I couldn't scrape by without his child support, but because without it, the kids would have to leave their private school.

They'd already lost their home and the kids they'd grown up with. I wasn't going to allow them to lose their school and friends there as well.

I made short order of clearing the dishes and took the stack to Mark. "You don't have to clean up," I said.

He laughed. "I have literally cleaned up after pigs. This is a piece of cake." He laughed. "Go back out. I'll be there in a second."

Haley came back down with Olivia and a much cleaner Bitty. With some sort of inner-radar, Mark came back out of the kitchen.

Olivia went to get Hilary, who did not look overly enthused to be rejoining us. We all watched as Bitty tore into her presents with help from Haley and Jeremy.

"Hey, Bits, let's see what Mr. Mark got ya," Jeremy said.

Haley nodded. "It's the biggest one."

They helped her tear the paper off and found a wooden rocking horse.

"She might be a bit too small for it," Mark said. "I had one when I was a kid. But maybe I should have made it the Millennium Falcon instead?"

"Nah, she can be a cowgirl," Jeremy said. "A space cowgirl."

He leaned over as if he was going to lift her up, but I hurried over and lifted her onto the horse for him.

Bit didn't understand rocking the horse, but she squealed with happiness at the new perch, then went back to her presents.

As she finished unwrapping gifts, I realized just a year ago, I was waiting for Alan to come home when Olivia showed up on my doorstep.

In just those short twelve months she'd become my family. I couldn't imagine my life without her and Bitty in it.

I looked at Alan.

And frankly, I couldn't imagine my life anymore with him in it.

He'd broken my heart, but in the last twelve months, my heart had mended. Hearts were really amazing things. They always seemed to have room to love more people and they could heal even after they broke.

They could not only heal ... they could become stronger.

I didn't miss Alan at all anymore.

No, it was someone else entirely that my heart ached for.

I realized I'd pulled out my phone. I checked it more often than I'd care to admit. And sometimes, I thought I felt it vibrate, indicating a text.

Every time, I'd feel a moment of elation before I realized it was a phantom vibration, that there was no call or text.

I missed Callum.

Which was ridiculous.

I didn't need a man.

Nor did I want one. At least not now.

Maybe some day.

Maybe not.

Later that afternoon, the decorations were still in place, but the party was over. Mark had gone, Alan had taken all three kids out for pizza.

That's how he operated. He breezed in on occasion, did some grand gesture, then left the parenting to Olivia and me.

I tried not to be bitter about it. It wouldn't change anything. I'd change what I could, accept what I couldn't... and hope for the wisdom to know the difference.

And I hoped Alan would change.

I know that for years, I was the enabler. I didn't require anything from him at home. I took care of the kids and the house. I kept his life humming along. I reminded him of appointments and special dates. I shopped for him.

I wondered if I was partially responsible for the man he'd become?

It was a morose thought.

I glanced at the clock and got ready for work.

Hilary scowled at me as I walked through the open door into Olivia's living room. "I'm taking off."

Olivia smiled. "I'll text you when Alan comes home with the kids, just so you know they're back safe and sound."

"I'm sure they're going to be a handful tonight. First the party, then seeing their dad."

She smiled. "No problem. We've got it down to a science."

She did. On nights I was gone, she had a system. When all three kids were tucked in, she left the upstairs door between the two units open. She could hear all three kids as easily as I could.

"I know you do." I shot her a smile and a look I hoped she could read as good-luck. "Thanks."

She nodded and smiled back.

I left Olivia with her cousin. Hilary hadn't said more than a handful of words to any of us. I suspect she was saving them all up for when I was gone. I felt bad for Olivia, but anything I tried to do was bound to make it worse.

I left for work, wishing I could have done more.

Chapter Sixteen

Olivia

On the plus side: I come from a very small family.

There were times when I was younger that I wished I had a bigger family.

Being an only child left me in the spotlight far more than I was comfortable with. And I always imagined having a sibling who would be my ally.

Hilary was a close to a sibling as I was ever going to come, but right now, she didn't look very ally-ish.

She scowled when we heard Alice's front door shut because the door between our homes was still open. It generally was.

Hilary made it a point of walking over to it and shutting it.

"Hil, what is up with you today?" I asked, frustrated by her rudeness at the party.

When we were growing up, I'd known all her childhood crushes. I'd cheered when she'd landed one and patted her back when one broke her heart.

Hilary was a like a butterfly, flitting from one crush to another, one boy to the next. She rode waves of utter excitement then eventually plunged into the depths of utter despair. As we got older, our closeness faded. We went to different universities and when we graduated, she went home to work for my father.

I did not.

When I told my family about the baby, I knew my parents wouldn't be happy, but even though we weren't as close as we'd once been, I thought Hilary would have my back. She'd been noticeably quiet and absent.

And after I broke things off with Alan and was alone with a new baby, she'd remained quiet. She hadn't bothered to make the six-hour drive to see me in the last year.

It was really hard to remember our old connection.

"She is taking advantage of you," Hilary said, frustration in her voice. "How many nights a week are you stuck with her kids?"

"Three. She works three twelve-hour shifts a week. Sometimes I have them less if Alan takes them." I didn't add that was rare. Instead, I said, "But I'm not *stuck* with them. I love watching them."

I thought about last week when Haley wrapped her arms around my neck and said, *I love you*. Jeremy didn't echo her words, but he did hug me, too.

The kids were Bitty's siblings. They were my friend's children.

But they were much more than either of those things to me.

I loved them, too. Not because of either of those connections. I simply loved them for themselves. "I would do anything for them."

"And Alice exploits that," Hilary said.

"Hilary, I don't want to fight with you, but you have no idea what you're talking about. You can't just breeze into my home and—"

Hilary interrupted me. "Olivia, this isn't your home. You could buy five places like this if you weren't so stubborn about your trust."

I wasn't surprised that my father told her that I wouldn't touch the money.

"It's not my money," I said. "I did nothing to earn it."

Hilary looked as if she'd like to pound her head against the wall. "Olivia, it's time to come home. Aunt Pauline and Uncle Emerson are willing to overlook your sit—"

This time I cut her off. "Seriously, Hil? You're seriously going to tell me that my parents will *overlook* my situation? Which situation is that? My affair with a married man or my out-of-wedlock child?"

I lowered my voice with effort. "Let's be honest, I never expected anything different from them. My mother has built her life on *overlooking* my father's indiscretions. And truly, what could my father say to me? Anything would come out rather like the pot calling the kettle black, don't you think?"

"Olivia," she scolded, sounding more like my mother than the cousin I'd grown up with.

"I'm worried about you," she said softly. Finally—in those words—I heard the cousin who'd once been my confident and faithful cohort beneath the high society woman she'd become.

"Hil, I love my life. I don't worry about country club gossip. I don't have to live up to anyone's standards but my own. I know that my friendship with Alice might seem odd to other people, but she is truly one of the most genuine, loyal friends anyone could ask for. I'm so lucky to have her. And for the record, she takes Bitty for me during the day so I can work."

"But you don't have to work," Hilary pointed out, once again sounding more like my mother than my cousin.

"You're wrong. I absolutely have to work. I don't want the life my parents had." I almost added, *the life you have*, but held that part back, but from her expression, I was pretty sure enough of our old connection remained and Hilary knew what I was thinking.

"Hil, my mother turns a blind eye to my father's affairs. She worries more about her social standing than ... well, anything else. Me? I worry about Bitty learning to crawl out of her crib. I worry that I will never be able to be everything my daughter deserves. But I know that I'll try to the mother she deserves."

Hilary sighed. "But I—"

I took my cousin's hand. "Hilary, why don't you spread your wings? You could come stay here with me until you find a place of your own. You could do anything, be anything." I didn't add that she didn't have to be my mother's clone or my father's protégé. I didn't mention all the old dreams she'd shared with me. She'd planned to take a year off to see the world and then go into business and conquer the world. "You don't have to stay with them."

"Someone has to," she said. "You left. You turned your back on them. I can't do that. I owe them—"

"Nothing. You don't owe them anything. You don't owe me anything either. But Hilary, you do owe yourself a chance."

"A chance to what?" she asked.

I looked at her and ached for her. My family might think my life was a mess, but I felt more at home here in this life I was building for myself than I'd ever felt there with them. I'd found where I belonged and I was building a life I loved.

"Hilary, you owe yourself the chance to be ..."

"To be what?"

"Whatever it is you were meant to be," I said softly.

"Maybe this is it. Maybe this is all I was every meant to be."

"I don't believe that," I said.

But I saw that she did. She believed she was all she was meant to be.

Quietly, I added, "And until you believe it, too, I'll just believe for both of us."

Chapter Seventeen

Alice

On the plus side: Pain can be eased by a friend's understanding.

After an awkward afternoon partying with an I-don't-want-to-pay-child-support ex, I was hoping for an easy, quiet shift at work.

I deserved an easy night.

Sometimes my twelve-hour nights were indeed easy.

When I looked at my assignment, I saw that I only had one patient, for half a moment I thought just maybe I'd pull it of. But when I saw who my patient was and I felt that hope wither.

Jemma Martone was one of those patients I couldn't seem to maintain a professional distance from. Maybe it was the fact she was only twenty-one. Maybe it was she reminded me of Haley. They both had dark blonde hair and I'm sure most people would believe they were related if they saw them together.

Maybe it was the tragedy of it all. She was walking home from the library when a drunk driver hit her. Such a wasted life.

Maybe it was knowing Jemma wasn't going to make it.

Or maybe it was all that added to watching her mother's grief deepen with every day that went by. Watching her mother's slim hope finally fade to quiet resignation. Every day knowing she was one day closer to losing her child.

I'd told Callum all those weeks ago that hospitals could be a *plus side*...that most of the patients left healthier than they arrived. That was true.

But some patients wouldn't.

Jemma wouldn't.

She'd been on my floor for a week. She'd never been conscious. Never spoken a word to me. Yet I knew I was too wrapped up in her case.

Sue Martone arrived every morning as soon as visiting hours started and didn't leave until we prodded her to in the evening.

Some patients' families couldn't be persuaded to leave. We'd had a woman a few months ago who spent every minute at her husband's side. We tried to encourage Addie Grayson to go home and get some rest, but Mark found her preparing to spend the night at the hospital chapel.

I'd bent the rules for her. And to be honest, I'd become as wrapped up in Gray and Addie as I had with Jemma and her mother, Sue.

Maybe with Gray and Addie I saw a couple on the brink and longed for them to make it...in a way Alan and I couldn't.

With Jemma, I felt her mother's pain. Just imagining that it was Jeremy, Haley, or Bitty in that bed tore at me.

When visiting hours were over, I walked into the room and nodded.

Sue saw me, stood up and kissed Jemma's forehead. "I'll be back in the morning, sweetheart" she said.

As we left the room she said, "You'll call if..."

She didn't finish her question, but I nodded.

"I can be back in ten minutes," she said.

"I'll watch her," I promised, not as a nurse to a patient's family member, but as one mother to another mother.

As I checked Jemma's vitals the next time, I had a sinking feeling.

It was shortly after ten that night when the monitor started dinging and the yellow light started flashing. Jemma's pulse increased and her blood pressure dropped, confirming my feeling.

I still called the doctor and talked to him, knowing what he would say. As soon as I hung up from him, I called Sue Martone.

"Come back," I said simply.

Less than a half hour later, she entered the room at a run, I knew that keeping a professional distance was impossible.

At ten fifty-two p.m. Jemma Martone's heart slowed further. I turned off the monitor.

And I held Sue Martone as Jemma's heart finally stopped.

"She's gone," I whispered, not that loud noises could disturb Jemma.

Sue nodded and clutched at Jemma's lifeless hand.

"Is there anyone I can call for you?" I asked.

I'd asked before, but Sue had always said no.

She said the same this time.

So I sat with her, thankful that I didn't have any other patient to pull me away. I'd been asked before why I chose nursing instead of becoming a doctor.

This is why.

As a nurse, I could connect to patients and their families in a way a doctor couldn't. Being a nurse meant that tonight I could be there for Sue.

"It's always been just Jemma and me. Her father..." She shrugged. "He was never a part of our lives. I always thought someday he'd realize his mistake and he'd have time to get to know what an amazing person we'd created, but now..."

She was silent a few minutes, then said, "He wasted his chance. He'll never know her. I have so many memories. I think they'll help me find a way to ... Well, not move on. But maybe keep going. I'll remember when Jemma was ten. I got called into the principal's office because she'd been fighting. He was telling me about their zero tolerance policy and she was going to be suspended for two days. I ignore him and asked her what happened. Jemma said the class bully had smacked one of the slower boys. I'd called the principal in the past about that particular bully, but nothing got any better. Jemma was frustrated and rather than report him again, she walked up to that much bigger kid and decked him, then gave a hand up to the other boy and took him to the nurse's office."

"And they suspended *her*?" I asked, incredulously.

"Yes. I high fived her in front of the principal and told her we were going to go on adventure as long as she had the time off. My boss was great and gave me the two days off. We drove to Cook's Forest and stayed at a hotel and spa. We got our first pedicures and went canoeing down the river. That was the most trouble she ever got in at school. I didn't condone violence, but ..."

"She sounds like she was a very special girl."

Sue nodded and finally started to cry.

And because I knew that professional distance had long since blown out the window, I cried with her.

By the end of my shift, I was exhausted, which was par for the course, but it was compounded by the fact I was emotionally drained.

I needed a moment to catch my breath. A moment to find a place to tuck away Sue's pain.

Someday, I wondered if all the moments I'd tucked away would come flooding back. If they did, I wasn't sure I'd survive it.

So I dutifully tucked away good moments to counterbalance those bad ones. That's how my plus-side game had been born.

For instance that moment when Addie and Gray left the ICU, that was a good moment. Whatever had separated them before had been resolved. They left as a unit. The kind of couple you knew would be together for the rest of their lives.

What made one couple so strong and another couple so easily broken?

If I could figure that out, maybe I'd have a chance at a lifelong relationship someday. It wasn't going to be with Alan. And Callum … well, it had been too early to think about forever, but even another day of our odd relationship was out of the question after he met my kids. It was apparent he wasn't coming back. And without him, my morning coffee breaks had lost their allure.

I finished my shower and realized that I wasn't going to let Callum rob me of my coffees.

This morning I was reclaiming my fifteen minutes.

After my last couple months absence, it felt odd to walk to the coffee counter rather than to the parking garage.

Serena smiled when she saw me. "I've missed you. Sometimes you don't realize that people have become part of the rhythm of your life until they're gone. That's when you notice that there's a hole in your day."

"Sorry," I said.

I knew what she meant. I'd missed this. Not just Callum … *this.* My few minutes escape in the mornings. "Life got in the way."

I hadn't let Alan make me bitter and I wasn't going to let Callum take away something I enjoyed. In one of his books, Richard Bach said something about every problem brings a gift. Maybe this last year had taught—well, was teaching—me that my needs mattered. That I was strong enough to reach out and grab what made me happy.

That's what I'd done with Olivia and Bitty.

And while I missed Callum, that's what I was doing now. Taking back something that I wanted...no needed.

"I hope I see more of you." Serena said as she handed me a coffee.

I'd been so lost in my thoughts, I'd forgotten for a moment where I was.

"Thank you," I said, sliding a five across the counter. "As of today, I'm back."

Serena looked at my money shook her head. "This one's on me. Consider it a bribe to make sure you're back."

"Thanks, Serena." I tucked the bill in her tip jar and started for my normal table, but I couldn't sit there. So I sat at the next one over.

My cellphone rang before my first sip. It was Alan.

"Is something wrong with the kids?" I asked.

"No. I just talked to Olivia. I'd have called later, but both of you are wrapped up in the kids all the time and it's hard to talk."

Part of me wanted to say something snippy, like maybe he needed to be more wrapped up with his kids, but I held my tongue. Maybe that was another lesson I'd learned in the last year, sometimes words meant everything and sometimes they didn't help at all. There was a sort of wisdom in knowing the difference.

Alan continued, "I need to talk to you. I'm hoping you'll be more reasonable."

I'd just been thinking I was stronger now than I was a year ago. I decided I was more patient, too. Patient, but firm.

I said, "If it's about child support, I won't be more reasonable. Let's be honest, you are the one who's not being reasonable. Alan, you are the kids' father. You have an obligation to help take care of them. All three of them."

"You two—"

I interrupted him. "Listen, if Olivia and I took the kids to daycare, you'd be on the hook for half of that. But we juggle it between us. Consider that your child support break."

"You are not being reasonable," he said again in that patronizing tone of his.

"Alan, I have been nothing but. The kids have been through so much turmoil. I won't pull them from their school, and without your help, I'd have to. So if you want an easement in your obligation, then have your lawyer contact my lawyer."

I felt fairly confident that the court would agree that the amount of money he paid was fair.

"Alice, you have to—"

"Alan, we're divorced. I don't *have to* anything." And realizing there really was nothing more to say and feeling strong, I ended the call.

I dropped my phone next to my untouched coffee and put my head down in my hands.

Thoughts of Jemma, her mom, Alan, and my kids whirled around in my head and I felt tears well up in my eyes.

I blinked hard, fighting to keep from letting them fall.

I worried that if I started to cry I wouldn't be able to stop.

I might be strong, but that didn't mean that sometimes things just sucked.

Sometimes they sucked so much finding something for my plus side was next to impossible.

"Alice?"

I knew the voice, but didn't want to look up and see him. I purposefully kept my head down, staring at my coffee cup, hoping he'd take the hint and just keep walking, but I heard the chair next to mine pull out and then the rustling sound of someone sitting down.

"Are you okay?" Callum asked with such tenderness and concern that the tears almost escaped.

I blinked hard. "Of course. I'm fine. Why wouldn't I be fine?"

"You just look upset," Callum said.

"No, I look like someone who had a long night and is exhausted." I was being snarky, and he didn't deserve that. Even if he'd cut me off in a rather cowardly way, without offering a word of explanation, he didn't deserve to be my whipping boy.

"I didn't mean to disturb you," he said with a quiet dignity. He'd just started to rise when Serena appeared at the table, a cup of coffee in hand.

She set it down in front of Callum. "It's good to see you both together again. It seems like forever since you were a staple of my morning."

"Not forever," I said as Serena headed back to her counter. "Just two months."

I could have added *and four days*, but I thought that might sound pathetic. I clutched at my thoughts of the last year making me stronger and wiser.

Serena walked back to the coffee counter and I hoped that Callum would leave as well.

He didn't.

"I'm sorry," he started. "I should have called. I should have explained."

"Don't be." I was about to say something about some men weren't cut out to deal women who had kids ... Alan being a case in point. But I realized that Callum, unlike Alan, hadn't signed on for kids, so I added, "We didn't know each other long enough that you should have called or even shown up for coffee."

He looked as if he was going to say something more—apologize more—so I added hastily, "You didn't—don't—owe me anything."

"Then why do I feel as if I do?" he asked softly.

I didn't answer, because I didn't know what to say.

I'd been the one who put a limit on what we could tell each other, but we never ran out of things to say. Now that everything was out in the open, we couldn't seem to find enough words to fill up the growing void.

When we first met, coffee with Callum was enough to ease any bad night, but this morning it felt like his presence was magnifying everything I was feeling.

The pain over Jemma, my anger at Alan.

I was stronger than I ever thought, I reminded myself.

It didn't help.

"I should go," I said, feeling like I might break into true tears at any moment.

"You can cry without tears," he said out of the blue.

"Is that the voice of experience?" I asked.

Most men I knew would never admit to crying… even if it they were talking about crying without tears. But even after our time apart, I suspected that Callum wasn't most men and that admitting to crying wouldn't faze him.

"Listen, I miss you," he said instead of answering the question.

I felt a spurt of annoyance that we were back at square one. Back in a place where we didn't talk about anything that mattered.

I'd missed him. And two months ago, our anonymous morning coffees had been a pleasure.

I wasn't sure why being anonymous no longer felt pleasurable.

"Let's just have our coffee. We'll play catch up. What do you think about this season's…"

And we did.

But as I finished my coffee and made my way out to my car, I realized I didn't feel more settled.

As a matter of fact, I felt decidedly less than settled.

I got home and walked into total bedlam. Haley had just remembered she needed a toilet paper tube for art class.

When your first duty in the morning is unrolling a complete roll of toilet paper it's hard to brood about just why things didn't feel quite right.

As a matter of fact, when Callum texted me that night, I smiled.

Did you ever watch X-files? the screen asked.

No.

It's online ...

As I found the show, I realized that Callum and I were right back where we were two months ago.

And I again felt dissatisfied at the thought.

Chapter Eighteen

Olivia

On the plus side: You can only ever have one first date with a person. Which was a very good thing because one first date was torture enough.

I had a date.

I'd said those words to myself a dozen times since I started my day. It seemed like a very long time since I'd had an honest to goodness date.

And I hadn't been on a date since having Bitty.

Not only did I have a date, but I had to find a babysitter. That just added to the surrealness of my date.

I didn't have to look hard for a sitter. Alice offered to keep Bitty. To be honest, talking about my date was about the happiest I'd seen Alice since Bitty's birthday party.

Alan was being a doofus, but that was no shock.

Alan had been a doofus for a long time and it hadn't seemed to faze Alice.

No, it was more than Alan. Alice had gone to the funeral for a patient on Tuesday. A young girl whose death seemed to really be hitting Alice hard. She'd come to get Bitty after she got home from the funeral. When I'd finished work and walked into

Alice's living room, I found her rocking my sleeping daughter and crying.

She'd hastily brushed away her tear, but I'd seen them.

She'd jumped at the chance to take Bitty for an overnight. I think losing a young patient made her want to gather all the kids close to her. And Bitty was part of her kids.

It wasn't the first time the baby had spent the night away from home. Alan had taken her a couple times, and when I had the flu in the fall, Alice had kept her a few nights for me.

I knew that all I had to do was open the hall door between my place and Alice's and I could check on Bitty when I got home.

So it wasn't Bitty that I was worried or concerned about.

It was that I had a date.

The idea of a date shouldn't feel so alien to me.

I was only twenty-five. Most of my friends from college were just landing jobs in their chosen fields. They were scraping along, trying to pay college loans and find places to live.

They were driving old jalopies or maybe buying their first new car.

I'd never had to worry about scraping by or paying off loans.

When I was born, my grandmother set up a trust fund for me.

Oh, how I hated the sound of that.

The fact I'd never touched it for anything other than college tuition didn't alter the fact that it was there. I'd never go hungry or be without a home. Neither would Bitty. I felt a sense of comfort in that.

I could have easily bought a home of my own when Alice offered to rent me the other half of the duplex, but the idea of having Alice next door was appealing. I knew she needed my help with the kids. And at first I'd done it because I felt as if I owed her something, even though rationally I knew Alan had duped us both.

Now, I helped with her kids because I loved them.

But knowing I had money to fall back on set me apart from my peers.

Since I'd had Bitty, I'd realized just how spoiled I'd been. Even before I'd had the baby, I'd tried to break away from my parents and forge my own path.

Watching my father cheat on my mother time after time— watching my mother wither and die a little more each time he had a new girl on the side—was warping me.

I didn't want their life.

I'd tried to convince my mother to leave him. She'd be happier, I was sure, because frankly, I don't think there was a way she could be less happy.

But she wouldn't leave him. She preferred an awful status quo to an uncertain future.

So, I'd broken away from them both, but maybe not as far as I'd thought.

Since my Alan fiasco, I'd spent the last year psychoanalyzing myself. Maybe I'd been looking for a father figure when I'd started seeing Alan. He'd seemed so gentle and wise.

I realized in retrospect all those qualities I'd thought I'd seen in him had been manufactured in my head. In reality Alan had been a chip off my father's block.

Was I still as naïve now as I'd been then?

I stared at myself in the mirror.

I didn't think so, but then I hadn't thought so with Alan either.

Mark seemed like the genuine deal, but I worried that even if he wasn't, I wouldn't be able to spot his flaws.

In the weeks between Thanksgiving and Bitty's birthday, we'd begun a casual friendship. His father had been back in the hospital for a time, and Mark had been busy with him, the farm, and his volunteer work. So we texted.

I started to feel like Alice. Every time my phone binged, I felt a spurt of excitement, knowing it was probably Mark.

I'd never gone on a first date with anyone I'd spent so much time talking to. There was no reason to be nervous.

But maybe nerves didn't need a reason.

I finished dressing and needed some reassurance.

I walked next door. Alice and the three kids were sitting down to dinner. "Well?" I asked, twirling.

Alice nodded. "Very nice."

"Aunt Olivia you look like a movie star," Haley said.

My nervousness dissipated slightly at her assessment. "Why thank you, Haley."

"I like you better in jeans," Jeremy grumbled.

I knelt down next to him. "Me, too."

"Then why are you going out on a date with Mark? You could stay and have supper with us. Mom made enough," he offered.

I didn't remind Jeremy that he liked Mark. That the couple times Mark had come over, Jeremy had been thrilled. Instead I knelt down next to him. "Jeremy, it's just a date."

He shook his head. "No, it's not. You'll go fallin' in love with him and then he'll make you move away and take Bitty and then everything will change *again*."

That word *again* was so heartfelt it broke my heart. I could feel Jeremy's longing for the status quo. I'd love nothing more than to promise him that Bitty and I would always live next door, but he was smart enough to see through such hollow promises.

"Jeremy," Alice started, but I shook my head.

"You don't want anything to change," I said, rather than asked. "I get that, sweetie. I love being here with you and your mom and Haley. Bitty's so lucky to have you for her big brother and Haley for her big sister. I'd like to tell you that it'll be okay, that things won't ever change, but I'd be lying and we'd both know it. Everything changes. Someday you'll graduate from high school and move on to college or a job."

"Yeah, but then I'd be leaving, not you," he said with the logic that only a ten-year-old can have.

I smiled. "I'm going to tell you a secret, it's not any easier leaving than it is being left. And while I can't promise that we'll always live here together in this house, I can promise that no matter what, you'll always have a home with me. You, Haley, and your mom aren't just Bitty's family. You're my family."

"But we're not really," Jeremy said.

"I have this friend. She's a teacher and she married a man who was adopted. All the kids in his family were adopted. None of them were related by blood, but they were an amazing family. I met them at a party. They didn't look alike at all, but if you saw them, you knew they were a family. They were connected. That's what we are. A family. Your mom's like a sister I never had, so that makes you and Haley my nephew and niece. It doesn't matter where any of us go, we'll still be connected. Because even when families move or change, they're still…" I couldn't decide how to end my profound statement.

But I didn't need to. Jeremy smiled. "They're still a family."

"Yes."

"Okay, but Mark better be nicer to you than Dad was."

"Jeremy—" Alice protested.

We both had made a valiant effort to not badmouth Alan. But how exactly did you explain to a ten and nine-year-old that they had a new sister, who had a different mom?

The answer was, *awkwardly.*

"I might just be a kid, but I know that Dad wasn't nice to you or Mom. If Mark's not nice, then you just come home."

I kissed his forehead. He was too old for that kind of thing normally, but tonight he didn't fuss. "I promise, I will. You're right, I deserve someone who's nice to me."

"Have fun," Alice said. "We've got quite the evening planned here."

"Star Wars," Jeremy cried, looking happier now.

Bitty started to da-dum the theme and we all laughed. She had a long list of Star Wars noises. Her Chewbacca was beyond hysterical.

Suddenly, I wanted to stay and watch Star Wars again. I wanted to hear Bitty's sound effects and watch Haley and Jeremy's mock light saber battles.

As if she could read my mind, Alice said, "You've watched the movie as much as I have, so you know you won't be missing much."

She was wrong and we both knew it. I'd be missing them. I'd be missing being a part of the night's fun.

Still, I wasn't so rude that I'd ditch a man without good reason.

Mark and I had taken things very slowly. He'd come here, and in addition to texting we'd talked on the phone, but in the month and a half since Thanksgiving, we'd never gone out on a date. Just the two of us.

Staying home for a Star Wars night sounded so much easier than diving into the dating pool again.

Last time I'd dated it didn't end very well.

And yet, as I looked at my daughter, I knew that there was definitely one of Alice's plus-sides about my time with Alan.

"Have fun with that," I said. I leaned down and kissed Bitty, then Haley's head.

I'd no sooner entered my side of the house than the doorbell rang.

I opened the door and smiled at Mark.

"Wow, you look lovely," he said.

"So do you," I assured him. "Come in and let me grab my coat."

"It's weird to actually be going out together after all these weeks," he said. "I thought it would be easier. But I'm still nervous."

"Me, too," I confessed.

"I thought we'd go to Cloud 9," he said as I opened the coat closet. "My buddy says it's a great date restaurant. Really nice without being stuffy."

"That sounds wonderful—" I started, but was interrupted when his cellphone rang.

He pulled the phone out of his pocket and looked at it. "I'm so sorry, I have to get this."

He tapped the button and said, "Yes?"

He listened and then sighed. "I'll be there as soon as I can."

"I'm sorry, Olivia. I have to go home. It's my dad. I left Mrs. Bolivar there, but he's kicking her out and I can't leave him alone."

His father had been back in the hospital again a few weeks ago and needed supervised.

"I'll tell you what," I said. "Why don't you give me your address, run home and deal with your dad and I'll pick up dinner and meet you there. To be honest, I can go change into jeans and you can show me the farm while I'm there."

Having dinner in a kitchen and touring a farm sounded so much less intimidating than going out to a restaurant. I knew I was nervous, but I don't think I'd realized just how nervous until I was offered a way out.

"Are you sure?" Mark asked.

"As long as you don't mind me inviting myself over," I teased.

He leaned down and kissed my cheek in the most platonic way possibly, which made me wonder why I got a small shiver up my spine. "You are amazing."

"No. I'm just me. And I'm much more at home in jeans walking through your barn than I am in a dress."

He left me not only the address and instructions to call if I had problems driving the country roads in the dark. Then he bolted. He'd made other comments about his father that led me to believe that Mr. West was not the easiest man to get along with.

I called Cloud 9, canceled our reservation and explained the situation. They didn't have a takeout menu, but the maître d' was sympathetic and promised to have three of their steak dinners—a specialty—waiting for me when I swung by. I changed into jeans and a wool sweater, grabbed my Wellingtons and tossed them in the back of the car, before I picked up our dinner.

It was a thirty-five minute drive out through Wattsburg, a small town to the east of Erie, but most of the drive was on Route 8, a rather major road. We'd had a mild winter. The streets were clear, though the yards and fields were still snow covered.

My car smelled of pepper as I listened to James Taylor croon about country roads. I couldn't see much of the scenery because six p.m. in January was dark, but I did see a group of deer to the right of the road as I drove. I slowed down, knowing they could be unpredictable.

As I pulled into Mark's driveway, I realized I'd forgotten to be nervous. Somehow takeout while wearing jeans didn't seem nearly as date-like as a restaurant in a dress.

Mark stepped out in the driveway as I got the take out containers out of the car.

"Wow, you were seriously hungry," he said with a laugh.

"I am seriously planning to sit down at the table and enjoy a meal where I don't have to shovel every other bite into someone else's mouth. Bitty is demanding. And frankly, she finds my food so much more appealing than hers."

He laughed. "I promise, I can manage my dinner on my own."

He ushered me inside. There was a small mudroom that had hooks on the wall and a big chest and then a second door that led into the kitchen. It was a kitchen that looked as if no one had ever updated it. If it had been a house from the sixties or seventies that was all funky colors and Formica, the lack of updates might be an issue, but this was an original farm kitchen. Straightforward wooden cabinets, wide planked wood floors and some sort of greyish stone counter and sink that was a deeper grey. Only one wall had upper cabinets, the wall over the sink/counter area had a wall filled with cast iron pans just hanging from nails.

And where a modern home might have an island, Mark's kitchen had a large butcher block.

"Wow, this is lovely," I said. I could picture Mark's mother and women from earlier times than hers bustling about this room, making meals for their families and farm hands.

Mark looked around as if trying to see what I was seeing. He obviously couldn't quite manage it because he said, "I've told Dad we should update it."

"Don't you dare," I said. "People pay huge amounts of money to make their modern kitchens look like this." I set the dinner containers down and wandered through the kitchen. I stopped at some large cast iron press thing on a shelf. "What's this?"

"It's a fruit or sausage press," Mark said.

"It was made in Erie at an old cast iron plant. Griswold," said an older man standing in the doorway.

Well, standing was a generous description. He was hunched over a walker, as if decades of work had permanently bowed his back, but as his eyes met mine, I saw that those same years hadn't bowed his spirit in the least. "My father worked at the plant for years," he said.

"Mr. West? I'm Olivia." I held out a hand and he let go of his walker and shook it.

"I'm Tyler. Tyler West."

"Would you like to join us for dinner?" I asked.

"Can you cook better than Mark?" he asked.

I shook my head. "Probably not. Okay, no *probably* about it. I am not a cook. Everyone at home assures of that. But I can do take out like a pro."

He barked a sound that I was pretty sure was rusty laughter. "That sounds good."

"Hey, your turkey was good," Mark staunchly defended me.

"Turkeys are so big, I think they leave a lot of room for mistakes," I said.

Mr. West sat down at the table.

"Dad," Mark said.

"That's his polite way of telling me I'm butting in on his date. My son is the soul of politeness." Mr. West made that sound like a bad thing.

"I'll tell you what?" I said, hoping to keep the peace between father and son, because there was a tension radiating between them that was almost palpable. "You join us for dinner, and then butt out when Mark takes me on a romantic tour of the farm afterwards." I said it teasingly, hoping to jolly both men out of their silent fight.

"There's nothing romantic about a farm," Mr. West said. "It's hard work. Of course, some people don't care for doing a real day's work."

"It's hard work for you guys," I said quickly in order to keep Mark from rising to the bait. "I'm just a tourist, so I can find it romantic if I like. Sort of like this kitchen. It's obviously a room where a lot of hard work is done, but as someone who came in carrying takeout, it's simply a very picturesque kitchen."

Mark set out the to-go boxes and I pulled out a bottle of wine. "It's from Presque Isle winery," I said.

"I don't drink," Mr. West said firmly.

"I'm so sorry, I should have asked," I said.

"It's fine," Mark said. "I can open it for us."

I shook my head. "No, let's just eat."

Neither man spoke directly to one another as we ate. I felt like the fulcrum in what became a seesawing conversation.

"Tell me about Griswold," I said to Mr. West.

"It was around for almost a hundred years. A lot of the cast iron on the wall came from there. It still works and..."

When he ran out of things to say about the now defunct Erie company, I said, "Mark, tell me about the farm."

He told me about the flock of chickens and his handful of pigs and cows.

"Back when I ran things, we had a lot more here, and we didn't worry about Mark's hippie dippy organic rules."

"It's about stewardship, Dad," Mark said. "We might not have as much going on here, but what we do have is sustainable. It's healthier and—"

"Bah," Mr. West said eloquently.

I jumped in. "I was just reading an article about a new project in Erie. The Greenhouse. Its goal is to promote sustainable..." and I kept chattering about the article, about taking the kids to go tour the Greenhouse.

"You have kids?" Mr. West asked.

"A daughter. And two more who aren't mine, but live with me. Well, by me. It's complicated," I ended awkwardly.

"Most of life is," Mark said with a sigh.

I helped clean up. Mark announced we were going for our tour.

Mr. West stood up. "It was a pleasure meeting you, Olivia. I hope you come out to the farm again soon. You can bring the kids. The one who's yours and the others who aren't."

"It was nice meeting you, too, Mr. West. And thank you. The kids would love it here."

"Clean up is definitely on the plus side when you order take out," I said as we made quick work of the dishes.

"I've heard Alice talk about plus sides," Mark said.

"I got it from her," I said. And not for the first time, I realized how much I had learned from her about parenting and life in general. "I swear she can find the silver lining in just about anything."

"Would you like that tour now?"

"I would. Is your dad okay in the house by himself."

"Yes."

I put the bottle of wine back in my car as got out my Wellingtons and pulled them on.

"So?" I said.

Mark led me towards a barn at the back of the property. There was a light over the door so I could see that it was painted a faded red. There was a large door on a track with a smaller regular-sized door in the middle—we went through that.

It was decidedly warmer in the barn than outside. It smelled of animals, but not in an unpleasant way.

Mark started to recite facts with the efficiency of a Hollywood tour guide.

"Mark," I said gently. He was avoiding talking about his father. As someone who tended to avoid that very subject, I understood, but a superficial date wasn't what I was after.

"I'm so sorry that the date was ruined," he said.

"First dates are about finding out about each other. And while I love hearing that this farm has been in the family for generations, I'd like to hear more about you."

He was quiet, so I added, "Here's the thing, finding time to date is going to be hard," I added hastily. "But if I'm taking time away from the baby to date, it has to have some substance. Do you understand? If all you want is some frivolous, superficial date, there are websites for that."

He sighed. "That's not what I want. And I do understand. My father might resent needing my help, but he *does* need it. It's tough to juggle for me, too."

"So while we both have the time, let's talk about something more than what type of chickens you're raising."

He sighed. "What I'm hearing is that talking about my free range chickens is not going to distract you from asking what's up between me and my father?"

"I'd like to point out that I didn't ask about that, but it was obvious that something was up."

"We have a long, complicated relationship."

"There's that word again," I said. I sat down on a hay bale and patted the space next to me. "Mark, I think everyone has complicated relationships with their family. Even if it's a good relationship, it's complicated."

He sighed and sat down next to me. "He doesn't drink because he's a recovering alcoholic."

I'd guessed as much. "Then I'm even more sorry I brought wine into the house. It won't happen again."

He shook his head. "You didn't know. To be honest, I don't think many people know. I didn't for a long time. He was a functioning alcoholic. But he didn't function well enough to manage the farm. It was on the brink of foreclosure when I bought it. If he'd told me sooner, I'd have helped him, but asking for help isn't something he does. Especially not from me. And of course, if you asked him, he'd tell you that he almost lost the farm because I didn't want to be a farmer."

"And yet, here you are, a farmer," I pointed out.

He offered me a wry smile. "I know. I went to divinity school and thought I'd be a minister with a church of my own someday. But instead I went into the military and spent five years ministering to the troops overseas."

For a moment there was such sadness on his face. If we knew each other better, I would have wrapped my arms around him, but we didn't. His hand was on the hay bale, next to his thigh, so I settled for placing my hand on his.

He flipped his hand so ours were palm to palm and he gave mine a squeeze. "When I came home, I was burnt out and I found out Dad was losing the farm, so I bought it. I'll confess I find solace here. Dad's still bitter. I tried to explain to him that it was never that I didn't want to farm, rather it was that I felt I had to do something else. But in hindsight, I think I had to do something else first. I'm content being here and doing what I do."

"And rather than a church, you volunteer at the hospital."

"Yes. For me, this works for now. Being outside here gives me... I don't know. Peace? It makes it easier for me to help people as a chaplain." He paused. "Your turn."

This was not a normal first date. I knew that. I wasn't going to tell him my sign, or where I went to college. He was asking for more than that. And I preferred it that way. "What did Alice tell you about our relationship?"

"Only that you're a friend and you two share the house. Of course, I was at the baby's party and know there's more."

I knew his answer before I asked. Both Alice and I had enough trouble explaining our friendship to family. We didn't tend to tell other people casually.

And while I hadn't lied when I said I didn't want to casually date Mark, I'd also been truthful when I said that if I was taking time away from the baby, I wanted something with some substance.

"It's more complicated," I started. "I was involved with Bitty's father. We were engaged and planning to be married after I had the baby." I waited.

Mark simply shook his head. "It happens."

"Aren't you supposed to admonish me or something?" I half teased.

He shook his head. "Not me. I tend to live by the thou-shalt-not-judge instruction. I have noticed a lot of people seem to miss that one."

I smiled. "I saw a text on Bitty's dad's phone and realized he was seeing someone else. Rather than confront him, I went to tell her to leave him alone. I was going to tell the other woman that he was taken."

Oh, how I remembered that night just over a year ago. It had been cold then, too. But also snowy. So snowy. If I hadn't been so outraged, I'd have never gone out.

I knew that I should have been outraged at Alan, even then. Before I knew who Alice was to him. Before I knew that he'd made *me* the other woman.

No, I couldn't blame Alan for that one. I'd made myself the other woman. Even not knowing he was married, I'd put myself in that position.

After all those years of knowing that my father was cheating on my mother and knowing she turned a blind eye to it, I swore I'd never let someone cheat on me. I hadn't bothered swearing I'd never be the-other-woman, because I knew that wasn't in me.

So much had happened in the last year.

"It wasn't until I got to Alice's house and saw Jeremy that I realized that she wasn't the other woman ... I was."

"Oh." Mark, paused a moment, then said, "Oh," again, understanding what I was saying. "I knew he was all the kids' dad, but I thought ..."

"You thought I'd seen him after they broke up." I shook my head. "Alice should have kicked me to the curb last year at this time. Instead, she kicked Alan to the curb and took me to the hospital and stayed with me as I gave birth."

I remembered the pain, but only in the most academic sense. What I remembered the most was the feeling of love as I held my daughter. And I realized that whatever I'd felt for Alan had paled in comparison. As I held Bitty, I realized that I'd never felt the way I should have for Alan. Not the way you should feel about a man you were considering spending the rest of your life with.

But my daughter? I couldn't imagine another second of my life without her in it.

And Alice? "Rather than hating me, Alice turned me and Bitty into family. I don't think I've ever met such an amazing generous woman before. Sometimes I want to be catty to Alan, but I remember Alice's generosity and try to emulate it. She makes it look easy, but it's hard."

"She does make it look easy," he said, rather than commenting on what I'd told him. "What about your family ... your biological family?"

"That's probably more complex than my relationship with Alice and the kids."

"Are they in town?" he prompted.

"No, not Erie. The first time I've seen anyone from my family in the last year was my cousin Hilary's visit for Bitty's birthday. You met her, and she's probably the most likeable family member."

"Oh," Mark said again.

I laughed. "Definitely *oh*. My parents have never seen the baby, other than the pictures I've sent. They don't approve of my *lifestyle* is what they say, but I think what they really hate is they can't control me."

I didn't explain that they had tried to use the family money as a way to rein me in. Money. Social standing. Those were the things that mattered to my parents, and unfortunately to Hilary.

I wanted something different for Bitty ... and for me.

"I don't need you to say anything comforting," I told him. "I figured out a long time back that I couldn't make my family be the family I want. They are what they are and I can either accept them as such, or spend the rest of life being bitter that I didn't get the family I wanted."

"What kind of family did you want?" he asked softly.

"Well, before I met Alice, I might have said that the family I dreamed about was just a made-in-Hollywood kind of family. The kind where people care about each other. The kind where they help each other. The kind that didn't worry about what other people thought. Alice taught me that wanting a family like that wasn't some dream that could never be realized because she helped me create that kind of family for Bitty. If something happens to me, I know she'd look after the baby as if she were her own. She humbles me."

Mark reached over and slowly draped his arm over my shoulder. The barn was warm and I could hear animals moving around. We didn't talk any more. We simply sat together in the quiet evening.

And I knew that even if things didn't work out with Mark, I would remember this night and this man who'd simply accepted me as I was.

It was the best first date ever.

It was definitely a plus side.

Chapter Nineteen

Alice

*On the plus side: "If this is you looking middle of the road,
I don't think I could survive you going all out."*

After three weeks, it was apparent that Callum and I
couldn't go back to when real life took a backseat.

It wasn't working. At least not for me.

When Callum hadn't known about my kids, it was fine. But
now that he did, not talking about them felt awkward.

Haley, Jeremy, and Bitty were my pride and joy. They were
at the center of everything I did.

Last night had been a quiet shift at the hospital. Normally
that was a good thing, but the silence left me plenty of time to
think. Too much time to think about Callum and me.

By the time I went down for coffee, I knew what I had to do.

Knowing what needed to be done didn't always make it
easier to do it.

We got our coffees and moved to our table, just like we had
so many mornings.

"How was your night?" Callum asked with a smile.

I could have simply answered that it was quiet. I could have stretched out this last coffee together and savored it, but I was tired of beating around the bush. "This isn't working."

Callum set his coffee down and didn't protest. Instead he nodded sadly. "I know and I can't figure out why it's not working anymore. It worked before."

Because I'd just spent an entire night thinking about our relationship, I had an answer, for what it was worth.

"*Before* we existed in a little bubble that insulated us from real life. We talked about things, yes, but nothing of any importance. It was simple. Easy. But my kids...they're my world. Though they're not simple and they're not easy. And the woman who brought them in that morning? She's more than a best friend. She's family. And our friendship isn't simple or easy. I can't pretend those complicated parts of my life away because they're at the heart of everything I am—everything I do. I thought we were done, and I was getting over losing you. And believe me, I know that losing you shouldn't have left much of a hole, but it did. Now you're here, but we can't go back in our bubble and we don't seem to be able to pull our relationship into the real world." I shrugged.

I was going to have to break things off with Callum. "I—"

"Why?" he asked.

"Why what?"

"Why isn't your relationship with your friend simple?"

"She was my husband's mistress. Though she didn't know it. She thought *I* was his mistress and..." I paused. "See, not simple. Definitely not easy. To be honest, it's all very messy. And Callum, I get the feeling you don't want messy."

"Then why can't we go back to what it was before? Why can't we be just Callum and Alice again?"

"That's what I spent my night thinking about. It comes down to the fact that you can't put the genie back in the bottle. We lived in a fantasy world, and now we're in the real world. And the real world is messy and difficult. If you'd asked me right after my divorce, I'd have said easy was fine with me. But it's been a year and I've healed. We built a relationship on ... well, words. We existed between the words. We talked about surface things. Movies. TV. Books. But between those words it's harder to pin down. The meanings are wispy and tenuous. Sometimes you can define what they are, but most of the time, they're beyond definition. It's beyond your ability to grasp. It's between words. You and I ... we could do the words and the concrete, but I don't think we're good at the ephemeral things."

"You want a relationship?" Callum asked, sounding confused. I didn't blame him. Those words had seemed so wise and profound last night, but they sounded more confused in the light of day.

"I'm not looking for a relationship. I'm not sure I could give it my all and still take care of the kids and give them what they need, but I know I'm not willing to settle for fantasy. To be honest, I think that's what my life with my ex was based on ... a fantasy. I saw what I wanted to see in it. He was never really the man I thought he was."

Callum looked uncomfortable. I could see it and I didn't blame him.

"It's okay," I told him. "We tried and we simply don't work in the real world."

I paused. "But thank you. For a while, that bubble we existed in gave me ..." I hesitated because I wasn't sure what it had given me, but I knew it helped heal me. "Thank you."

I started to rise, but Callum reached up and took my hand.

"Alice, I don't want to lose you. I don't want to lose what we've started."

I shook my head. "That's the point, we're not starting, we're trying to go back and that won't work. It's like when you're a kid and you believe in Santa and then you find out he's not real. After that, no matter how much you try, or how many times you watch *Yes, Virginia*, you know he's not real."

Callum pulled out his cell phone and set it on the table.

"I wrote you a text a couple days after your kids came in."

"You didn't send it?"

He shook his head. "I thought about sending it a dozen times a day, but I never did."

"What did it say?"

"*I miss you.*" He looked at me and I nodded. I'd missed him, too. "I never wanted kids. I avoid dating women with children."

"Why?" I asked.

"I've never been around them. I don't know what to do with kids."

I thought there was more to it than that, but I didn't push. I was pretty sure I'd pushed enough for now.

"I'd say come over, but I would never do that to ... the kids," I finished with a grin.

"Let's try the real world Callum and Alice. You're not sure if you have time, and I'm not sure I can make a go of it with a woman who's a mother." He shook his head and shot me a wry smile. "I know how awful that sounds. Like I'm the kind of guy who kicks puppies or something. It's not that I hate kids or anything. I just ... I know I don't want to walk away from you yet."

I wasn't any more sure we could make a go of it than he was, but I didn't want to walk away from him yet either. "If we're going to try the real world, let's start slow. I think you were about to ask me out on a date before Olivia and the kids interrupted that day."

"I was," he said.

"So ask me now."

"Alice, would you like to go out on a date with me?"

"Yes. But I will warn you," I said.

"About?" he asked.

"I haven't dated anyone in a very long time."

"Then I'll have to come up with something special."

He stood and held out his hand. "I'm Callum Gibson. Nice to meet you."

I stood and held out my hand. "Alice Collins."

"So, Friday night?" he asked.

"My ex has the kids on Saturday. Would that work?" I countered.

"Yes. I'll text you the details."

I nodded.

We were in the real world now.

And I was nervous.

That Saturday, *nervous* didn't even begin to describe how I was feeling. It felt as if every fiber of my being was pulled taut.

Nervousness, excitement, fear, hope … they all mixed into a swirl of emotions I couldn't even begin to sort out.

"Olivia, it's been since high school," I whined in a most unbecoming way.

If Haley had acted like this, I'd have scolded her.

But Olivia was the soul of patience. "High school?"

"I haven't gone out on a date with anyone but Alan since high school. That means I've never dated as an adult. I don't know what to do. I don't know what to wear. I don't know how to act. I need advice."

She thought about it a moment. "Let's see, the biggest advice I can give you is don't shave your legs before you go out."

Of all the things she might have said, this was not what I expected. I snorted. "What?"

Rather than answer, she added, "And wear your most awful, ugly granny-panties."

This time I laughed out loud. "Really?"

"Yes. If you haven't shaved your legs and are wearing ugly granny-panties, you won't be tempted to jump into bed with him after the first date."

I smiled. "Good point."

Although, even if I had on my best underwear and had smooth legs, I don't think I'd be tempted. I meant what I said, I didn't know how to manage an adult relationship.

"Did he say where he was taking you?" Olivia asked.

"No."

"So, wear something middle of the road. Black pants, a casual top, simple but classic jewelry. Something fancy enough for a nice restaurant, but casual enough to go ... bowling."

I laughed. "Good point. And even though you didn't mention it, no skinny jeans."

"Why?" she asked.

"Because if he's taking me bowling my feet would look like clown feet in those shoes if I had on skinny jeans."

This time she snorted. "I wouldn't have thought of that."

"You would if you wore size nine shoes," I assured her.

We laughed as I got out some dress slacks—not of the skinny variety—and held up a selection of shirts. Olivia kept shaking her head no and finally left and came back with shirts from her closet.

"I brought a few, but I think this one's perfect." She held out a white top that looked as if it just wrapped around. It was blousy and sheer, but not see through. And as I reached out and touched it, I knew this wasn't some acrylic or rayon top she picked up at the mall.

"Olivia?" I asked.

"There was a time when I wore things that weren't decorated with baby barf and boogers," she said simply.

Bitty had a cold and since she didn't understand what tissues were for, we were all covered in boogers on a regular basis.

I knew she had parents and other relatives. I also knew they'd all cut her off. Well, other than Hilary, who'd arrived wearing clothing like this. The kind of clothes that screamed *money.*

Although, Olivia was one of those women who looked perfect in faded jeans and oversized sweaters, I suspected she'd once worn another type of clothing. Maybe the ability to look well styled no matter what she wore came to her innately, or maybe it was something that came to her because of her upbringing.

Either way, I didn't have the ability.

Looking at the lovely top, I shook my head.

"I couldn't," I said. "I'd probably spill something all over it, or he'll take me bowling and I'll get it dirty and—"

"Try it on," she said. "It's just collecting dust in my closet. Mark and I are more prone to go traipsing through his barn than out to a fancy dinner. And really, I think it would be perfect on you," she added softly.

"Nothing's perfect," I said, reminding her as much as I was reminding myself.

"No, but some things come pretty close." She smiled in such a way that I knew she was thinking about Mark.

She'd gone out with him two more times since that first date. I didn't pry, but she seemed happy about it... about him.

I wondered if I'd look that moon-ish after a few dates with Callum.

I took the top and tried it on. I looked at myself in the mirror.

I didn't see Haley and Jeremy's mother. Or Alan's ex. Or Bitty's surrogate aunt. I saw someone I never really knew.

I'd been a girl when I'd dated Alan.

I wasn't her anymore.

Instead, I saw a woman staring back at me from the mirror.

I walked out and Olivia smiled. "Yes. That's perfect. Now, let me see about your hair."

An hour later, my hair was in a very simple looking chignon that had been anything but simple to style. I was wearing borrowed jewelry that Olivia insisted would be absolutely perfect with the outfit.

I fingered the pendent necklace nervously. I suspected it wasn't something she picked up at a mall and was scared to death I'd lose it. But Olivia wouldn't take no for an answer.

"You're kinda bossy," I said, imitating Jeremy.

"I think I've learned a thing or two the last year or so," she said with a laugh.

I glanced in the mirror again. "I don't think Callum is going to recognize me. Heck, I don't recognize me."

He'd only seen me after I'd showered in the gym. I generally had on yoga pants or jeans, and my hair was generally still damp and in a messy ponytail.

"You look lovely," Olivia said. "And don't forget—"

The doorbell rang.

"That's him," I said, feeling far more nervous than any adult should.

"Just remember two things. Have fun and granny-panties."

She ducked through the door that separated our homes and shut it.

I was still smiling when I opened the door for Callum. He was wearing tan slacks and a black coat that he'd left unbuttoned, with a simple sweater underneath.

"Come in," I said.

He stepped into the foyer, pushed up his glasses and smiled at me.

The house had a very small foyer. Actually, calling it a foyer was generous. It was a tiny tiled area in front of the closet. It worked well for wet boots, but if there were more than just the kids' and mine, it was too small. Tonight it was tidy, and thankfully so was the rest of the house.

If the kids hadn't been at Alan's all day, it wouldn't have looked this nice. Olivia and I laughed at ourselves because when he took all three kids, we both rushed around and picked up. The fact that a totally neat house was rare made moments like this all the sweeter.

It also made first impressions nicer too, I hoped.

"You look great," he said.

"Thanks. I wasn't sure what we were doing and Olivia suggested middle of the road—"

"If that's middle of the road, I don't think my heart could survive you going all out."

"That's today's plus side," I said, knowing he'd understand. "Thank you."

He smiled. "Being here with you … it's a plus for me, too."

We both stood there and smiled at each other for a ridiculously long time.

Finally, I said, "Did you want to come in first?"

He shook his head. "Let's just go."

"So where are we going?" I asked as I put on a coat.

"I thought we'd go to one of the North East wineries."

I nodded. "That would be nice."

We drove the half hour from Erie to neighboring North East, Pennsylvania along I-90. I caught glimpses of Lake Erie to the north from time to time. It gave me something to look at rather than staring straight ahead.

What I wanted to stare at was Callum.

We started at Presque Isle Winery, a small house on a hill overlooking a creek. I bought a bottle of a white bubbly wine. Maybe someday I'd open it for a special night with Callum.

If there were more nights with Callum.

We went further into North East to a newer restaurant, The Cork. He'd made a reservation, so we were seated right away.

The waiter left us with a menu and a wine list and Callum leaned toward me. "I just want to be clear. I know nothing about wines. I mean nothing to the point that I can't even fake know-ing about sniffing and swirling."

I laughed and felt as if the awkwardness shattered at the sound. "Me either. I bought the bottle earlier because I like bubbles. You could have faked it."

"Maybe we should just ask?" he said.

"Maybe. I think we both can agree we're no good at fak-ing it."

The waiter brought us each a glass.

"Nice," I said.

Callum agreed. "This is where we should get to know each other."

"Yes. Let's start with you. Did you grow up in Erie?"

He shook his head. "I was born in Toledo, and when I was seven, Mom and I moved here. She's in Texas now. She had fam-ily there," he added.

"And your dad?"

He got a funny look on his face. "I haven't seen him since I was six."

And from his tone and expression, he didn't want to talk any further about that.

I didn't push. I just nodded and he said, "Your turn."

"I was born in Erie and I've lived a lot of places but came back here for college. My mom's in…" I stopped to think. "Florida now. I don't talk to her often."

My childhood was one of rotating *father figures* and homes. I could hardly keep them straight. So much of my history was tied up with Alan's, so I didn't bring that up. It seemed like bad form to bring up a husband—even if he was officially an ex-husband—when you were on a first date. I couldn't think of anything else to say. I grasped for something and came up with, "School?"

"Penn State. You?"

"Gannon's nursing program. I did some internships at the hospital and they offered me a job when I graduated. I took a few years off when I had the kids, but I'm glad to be back at it."

I realized with that pronouncement we were officially out of our sheltered bubble and firmly in the real world.

"You're a nurse at the hospital?" he said slowly.

I nodded. "The nurse manager in ICU. You?"

"I work there, too. HR."

I felt a sinking sensation. "Is this a conflict?"

What if stepping into the real world meant that we had to stop seeing each other because of a work conflict?

"It's a big department. I don't deal with nursing staff, so no. Though I'll talk to my supervisor, just to be on the up and up," he said.

I felt an instant surge of relief. "I wondered if you were there in the mornings because you worked there or if you were there for *as* a patient or *for* a patient, but even after we started having coffee again, I didn't feel I could ask."

"Okay, new policy, no more dodging our real lives. Ask away," he said.

"Why HR?"

"I like trying to figure out what makes people tick. If you can figure that out, you can resolve a lot of conflicts before they happen. The hospital is such a big complex community...I think human resources has a lot to do with keeping it running smoothly." He paused, then asked, "Why nursing?"

"Maybe the same answer, but taken in a little different direction. Some of what I do is figuring out what makes people tick as well, I think. It's not just a personality or mental thing, but a physical one. I had a patient a while back who was in a medically induced coma. I swear, when his wife was there, his vitals were so much steadier than when she wasn't. Letting her stay with him as much as possible was good for him."

"So what you're saying is mental *ticking* can have an impact on physical *ticking*."

"Definitely." I paused. "Can I ask you something?"

"I think that's part of what dating is all about, asking questions," he said, waiting for me to ask.

"Why—" My question was interrupted by my phone. My ringtone was embarrassing, but Jeremy made it for me and I didn't have the heart to switch to something more conventional.

Here we go Otters, it rang.

We'd gone to a couple of Erie's local hockey team's games this season and Jeremy had taped the crowd chanting and turned it into a ringtone.

I glanced at the caller I.D. and picked up and asked, "Olivia. Is something wrong?"

She hesitated a second too long before she said, "Not exactly wrong, but…"

I heard someone shouting in the background.

"What?" I asked.

"Haley told Alan that you were going out to dinner with someone and Alan must have been complaining, because Jeremy's in a state. He says you're going to get a new husband and what if he doesn't like kids. Alan brought them home and said he'd stay to *reassure* Jeremy until you got home. I told him I thought he'd *reassured* Jeremy quite enough, thank you and kicked him out. I wouldn't have called, but…"

But Jeremy needed me.

Olivia didn't have to say it. I knew it. "No. I'm glad you called. Thank you. We're out in North East, so it will take a half hour or so to get home."

I could see Callum already trying to flag down our server for the check.

"Let me talk to him a minute though," I said, hoping I could calm him down a bit.

I heard Olivia trying to get Jeremy to come to the phone and heard him distinctly say, "No. Tell her I can live with Dad so she don't got to worry about me and can just kiss her *boyfriend* all the time."

I was going to do my ex in, I decided.

I'd worked so hard to be fair and magnanimous, but Alan seemed bound and determined to be a—I thought of a Jeremy term—a butt munch.

Olivia said, "Sorry. He—"

"I heard," I told her. "We'll be there as soon as possible."

I hung up and looked at Callum. "Sorry."

Back when I dated Alan, I hadn't had to deal with kids' issues.

Callum was just as nice as I thought he'd be. He shook his head. "I get it. I can't imagine it's easy on kids to have their mother date."

"They haven't had much experience with it," I said. "*Any* experience with it, if I'm completely honest. They were supposed to be with their father tonight, so I didn't explain or prepare them. That's my fault. I didn't think they'd ever know. But my daughter has a way of hearing things she shouldn't."

We hurried out and were flying down I-90 in short order.

"My mother never dated, but I can't imagine I'd have liked it any more than Jeremy does," Callum said.

"Never?" I asked. I knew I was hesitant about dating, but I'd never imagined that I would *never* date.

"Not to the best of my knowledge," he said. "My father did a number on her. I don't think she was eager to repeat the experience."

I nodded. "On the other hand, my mother dated a lot. To the extent that she was never precisely sure who my father was."

That was something I rarely told anyone.

Callum was quiet a moment and finally said softly, "There are times I wish I didn't know anything about mine."

I was about to ask him why when he suddenly changed the subject. "So what Harry Dresden book are you on now?"

I didn't press. Some things were simply too hard to talk about with ease. Letting them out slowly was the easiest way. It was kind of like a balloon. If you popped it, it was ruined, but if you let the air out slowly, it could adjust to its new dimensions.

We didn't have to share a complete autobiography tonight.

Talking about books was a great distraction. Soon, we were pulling up in front of the house.

The bayfront was lit up, casting a glow down below the cliff opposite of my house.

The lights on both sides of the porch were lit as well.

I could make out Callum's face. I reached up and gently touched his cheek before I got out of the car.

This man.

I'm not sure why, but he made me forget I hadn't dated in years.

He made me forget I was a mother with two children.

He made me forget that while I knew many things about him, I was just beginning to actually know him. I felt as if he'd been a part of my life for a long time.

"I would have invited you in tonight, but I'm not sure how worked up Jeremy is. I don't think it's good to fan the flames if we don't have to."

There were flames I would like to fan, but now was not the time.

"I understand," he said.

I could hear the relief in his voice and couldn't blame him in the least. Everyone talks about the *terrible twos*. That particular year seemed like a cakewalk in retrospect. I'd definitely say that the *tens* were far more terrible.

"Maybe soon?" I asked.

He nodded. "Yes."

I thought that was it, but before I could get out of the car, Callum pulled me into his arms and kissed me. And for that moment, I forgot again.

Finally he pulled away and reality came flooding back.

"I've been wanting to do that all night," he said.

"Me, too. It was nice," I said as I practically fled the car.

It was nice?

I groaned to myself as I walked up the walk to the porch then inside my door.

Nice? That was not the right word to describe how that kiss felt.

I shut the door, turned the lock and was greeted to the sound of... nothing.

It was suspiciously silent in the house.

Since it was only eight thirty, I was pretty sure the kids weren't asleep.

There were certain truths every parents knows... when the kids were awake and quiet, there was danger on the horizon.

"Hello?" I called.

There was nothing on my side, so I walked through the open door in the living room to Olivia's side.

She was rocking Bitty.

"Where are the kids?" I asked.

"They went upstairs. Jeremy is in a state. He said you must have kicked his dad out so you could go out on dates again. He told me if you'd only told his dad, Alan would have taken you on dates."

I needed to go upstairs, but first I needed a half a moment to prepare myself.

"What is wrong with Alan?"

"If you want my opinion, he's jealous," Olivia said. "He asked me about the guy I was dating. I know it's mean to think and even meaner to say, but I can't help but wonder if he's seeing more of the kids now so he can grill them on what we're both up to. He seemed very well informed."

"I seriously can't imagine why he'd care," I said.

Olivia stroked Bitty's hair, then looked at me. "Just because you don't want something yourself, doesn't mean you want someone else to have it."

I sighed. "It would be nice if he could be ... well, a little less *Alan*."

Olivia laughed. It wasn't her normal joyful laugh, but a cynical one. "I don't know that I'd hold my breath waiting for that to happen."

"I'll go upstairs and try to explain things to Jeremy." I knew as a parent I'd have uncomfortable talks with my kids. I anticipated talking about them dating one day when they were older. I had not imagined having to talk to a nine and ten year old about *me* dating.

It was still very quiet as I reached the landing.

I knocked on Jeremy's door. I could hear the kids, but they didn't answer, so I opened it the door.

Jeremy had my big suitcase on the bed, and Haley was wearing her Yoda backpack.

"Are we going somewhere?" I asked.

"I'm leavin'," Jeremy said, anger reverberating in his voice. "You don't want me and Haley anymore, so I'm going."

I wanted to cry and at the same time, I wanted to go kick Alan ... hard. I pushed back both emotions and managed to ask, "Where you are going?"

Jeremy shrugged.

"Your dad's?" I asked.

He shook his head. "Nah. He said he doesn't got enough room for us. So me and Haley, we're running away."

"I don't wanna go," Haley said in a small voice, "but Jeremy would be lonely without me."

I nodded. "Okay, give me a few minutes to pack and I'll be ready to go, too."

"Where are you going?" Haley asked.

My heart was breaking, but I forced myself to maintain a nonchalant attitude as I answered, "I don't know. Wherever you two are going, that's where I'm going."

"Mom, I can't runaway with you and Haley. Next thing you know Olivia and Bitty'll want to come."

"Oh, that's a great idea." I pulled out my phone and texted Olivia, holding it just so that Jeremy could see it.

Jeremy's running away. Haley's going with him. Me too. Wanna come?

None of us said anything as we watched the phone. A few seconds later, the phone beeped. *Would be too lonely here if you all left, so of course Bits and I are coming.*

Jeremy smiled slowly. "Okay, I get it."

"Get what?" I asked.

"You love me."

"Yes. And?" I prompted.

He looked blank, so I filled in for him, "And that will never change. I should have told you I was going out on a date, but dating someone means you're getting to know them. You never know if you'll go out on a second date or not. So I didn't want to say anything until I knew for sure."

"You wanted to know if you liked him enough to go out again?" Jeremy asked.

I nodded.

He mulled that over a moment as Haley took off her book bag and climbed onto my lap.

"I liked Carrie at the beginning of the year, but I don't any more. Like that?" Jeremy asked.

"Exactly like that. I'm not going to lie, I'll probably go on more dates. But here's the big thing you both have to remember.

No matter what. No matter who. No matter where. No matter when. I will always love you both more than pickles."

It was a game we used to play when they were smaller. A game that they'd altered as they got older.

"More than boogers?" Jeremy asked, with a reluctant chuckle.

I couldn't help but laughing as well. "Definitely more than boogers."

"How about Olivia and Bitty?" Haley asked.

"I love them, too. Maybe someday I'll date someone and decide that I not only like him, but I love him. If that happens, it'll still be okay. You know how I know?"

Jeremy shook his head.

Rather than answering, I asked, "When Olivia had Bitty moved in we all found out we loved them, right?"

"Yeah," both kids said.

I nodded my agreement. "But just because you love Olivia and Bitty doesn't mean you love me less, does it?"

Haley immediately shook her head, but Jeremy thought about it a moment. "Yeah, I guess I see. I love you and Dad and Haley, but I can love Olivia and Bitty, too. It doesn't mean I love you less."

"That's right. Love is magic."

"Like Harry Potter?" Haley asked.

"More magic than even wizards can do. You can never run out of love. You can give it away to your whole family and someday find someone else and love them…and still have love leftover."

"Yeah, that's magic," Haley agreed.

Slowly, Jeremy nodded. "I get it."

"I'm glad." I breathed a sigh of relief. Crisis averted.

"Listen, if you ever want to runaway, you let me know first. I'll pack my bag and go with you."

He smiled. "If you're gonna come with me, I guess I should probably just stay."

"Yeah. I think you probably should. Uh, someone should probably go tell Olivia not to pack."

"I will," Haley said, springing from my lap.

"Shh," I said. "I think Bitty was on her way to sleep."

"Okay," she said as she darted out the door. We both heard her clomping down the stairs.

"Mom, were you gonna bring that guy over?" Jeremy asked.

"I hadn't planned on it. At least not for a while."

He shook his head. "Nah, you shouldn't wait. I need to meet him."

"Let me think about it," I said.

"Okay, but if I meet him, I won't have to worry as much. I'll know if he's a good guy or not."

My son was too smart for his own good sometimes. He knew how to play the guilt card. "You don't have to worry at all."

"Sure I do. I know Dad was dating Olivia. I figured that out. And that's why Bitty's our sister. And I know that Dad shouldn't have done that."

"No, he shouldn't have. And though it wasn't a good thing, something good happened. We got Bitty and Olivia in our lives."

"Yeah, its kinda weird though, right?"

"Here's a secret. Every family is weird. Every family, no matter what they tell you, is weird in their own way."

"Sorry I was freakin' out," he said.

I shook my head. "Sorry I didn't tell you I was going out on a date up front. Do you want to talk about anything else?"

"No," he said. "I think I'm okay now."

I started to get up, but Jeremy threw his arms around my neck and launched us both backwards. We bounced on the bed and laughed as we hugged.

"I love you," I told him.

"I love you, too," he said.

Crisis averted, I thought again.

I got the kids settled and tucked in.

Then I texted Callum. *Sorry for the early night. I had a lovely time.*

Everything okay there? he replied

It's fine. Jeremy wants to meet you and check you out. Don't worry. I don't expect you to meet them yet.

I might have an idea. Let me look into it and I'll talk to you at coffee.

Ok. Goodnight.

Goodnight.

What I didn't say was that our kiss had been anything but nice.

I set down the phone and reached up and touched my lips.

No, that kiss was so much more than nice.

It was more than even a plus-side.

Chapter Twenty

Alice

On the plus side: A guy who pays attention to little things.

"I'm so sorry about Friday," I said as we sat down at our table. We had our coffees in hand and so much to talk about.

Oh, we'd 'talked' on the phone since our aborted date and I'd apologized then as well. In the history of first dates, I was pretty sure ours had been a bust.

Well, except the kiss.

The kiss part had been pretty awesome.

"Like I said, its no problem," Callum said. "I hope we can do it again soon."

I nodded, but before I could say anything, he went on, "And I have an idea."

"Oh?"

"I noticed your ringtone when we went out. You're an Otter's fan?"

I nodded. "Jeremy and Haley went to a game for a friend's birthday a couple years ago. They've been hooked ever since. And while I'm not the most sporty person ever, I'll confess, I'm rather hooked as well. Jeremy keeps trying to convince me to be a billet family."

Callum quirked his eyebrows.

"A lot of the kids who play for the team are young and away from home. So local families put them up and act as surrogate parents. I told Jeremy maybe someday, but not any time soon. I've got all I can manage right now."

It was nice to think that someday I'd be able to handle more. But right now, I felt as if my plate was full and if I tried to add too much more, I'd spill it all.

"Then my idea is better than I thought," Callum said. "I got an invitation from acquaintance to an Otters game. His company has a box and told me to feel free to bring a date. Before I talked to you, I called him and asked about bringing a date and her kids. He said the more the merrier."

"Oh, Callum, we couldn't intrude on your friend that way."

"Really, it's a corporate write-off. I met him because his company works with the hospital. Ash and I were partnered in a golf tourney last year and we've had a social friendship ever since. You'll like him. He's great."

I hesitated.

"Seriously," Callum said. "The kids will have a blast."

I laughed. "You had me at *the-kids*. You're sure though?"

He nodded.

"I'd like to talk about why you've never dated women with kids," I said. That he'd never been around kids, I understood. But I had a feeling there might be more.

He hadn't said he simply had never dated a woman with kids, he said he *didn't* date women with kids. There was a difference.

"I'm just not sure I'll be good with kids. But who knows, maybe they won't be good with me."

I smiled. I was pretty sure there was more, but I didn't expect Callum to share all his stories with me immediately. So I let it go.

"I'm sure they'll be over the moon."

Turns out the kids weren't over the moon. They didn't even make it out of the atmosphere.

"I don't wanna go with your boyfriend," Jeremy whined. Our talk the other night seemed to have been forgotten.

Whiney kids gave me hives.

"It's a box at an Otter's game," I said trying to sound more patient than I felt. "There's going to be pizza and soda."

Jeremy didn't look convinced.

And he was still complaining when Callum arrived.

I opened the door and he was there, with a bouquet of flowers. "Happy Valentine's Day," he said.

"Valentine's Day?" I repeated dumbly.

I'd bought the kids boxes of cards a few weeks ago for school, but I hadn't really registered the holiday. And I certainly hadn't thought about dating Callum on Valentine's. "You really shouldn't have."

He must have sensed my discomfort. "It's fine, Alice. They're just flowers. And really, we're going to a hockey game. I don't think that qualifies as an intimidatingly romantic sort of date."

I smiled and remembered my manners as I took the large bouquet from him.

Thankfully, they weren't roses. That would make me really uncomfortable, but I wasn't sure why. It was a large bouquet of mixed flowers. Not a rose among them.

I pressed my nose into them. "Thank you. Come on in and meet the kids. I'll just put these in water before we go."

The kids were still in the living room. Jeremy glared when he saw I was carrying the flowers. I tried to ignore his mood.

"Callum, this is my son, Jeremy and my daughter, Haley. Kids, this is Mr. Gibson."

"Nice to meet you," Callum said.

Jeremy scowled and Haley smiled.

Callum followed me into the kitchen as I filled the vase, cut the stems and placed the flowers in the water.

I smiled. "It was really sweet of you to think of Valentine's."

"To be honest, it might not have registered with me either, but Jill is just across the way from me at work. Her husband sent her a huge bunch of flowers today. It was hard to miss the holiday after that."

"Tell Jill thank you," I said.

He laughed. Then looked serious. "I'm sorry your son isn't happy."

"Part of me wants to do whatever I can to make him happy, and the other part of me wants to kick his butt for being such a puke. I've decided to ignore his pouting unless he's out and out rude."

"I'll follow your lead," he said.

We went back to the living room where Jeremy was still glowering.

I ignored his expression and asked, "Shall we go

Jeremy tromped to the car like a man on his way to the gallows.

"So, I'm not winning him over?" Callum whispered to me.

"He's not sure what to make of me dating. It's not you. It's me. And that is absolutely not just something I'm saying."

Callum laughed. "Yeah, I have to sympathize. If you were my mom, I suspect I'd have reacted like Jeremy."

"Still, I'm sorry," I said.

As a parent, I knew my kids weren't perfect, but I always hoped they would be.

"I might not know a lot about kids, but I can be understanding. I won't take it personally," he assured me.

We drove the dozen or so blocks from Front Street to the hockey arena. Callum parked in the ramp across from it.

When we got to the box, Callum introduced me to our host, Ashton Carlyle.

"Call me Ash," the handsome, tall blond said. "We're happy you were able to come, Callum. And Alice, it's nice to meet you. And these are?"

"Jeremy and Haley," I said.

"And this is my business partner…" Ash elbowed a man who had his back to us.

"Gray?" I said as the man in question turned to face us.

The woman next to him turned as well when she heard me.

"Alice!" they said together.

"Addie, Gray, it's so good to see you both."

I am not a hugger by nature. Sure, I hug my kids, but social hugging? Not for me. Still, I hugged them both.

A lot of patients and their families go through our unit.

It would be impossible to remember them all. But some stood out.

Gray and Addie were two of those people I would carry with me for a long time.

Gray looked so much better than the last time I saw him months ago. I didn't mention where I met him. HIPAA rules not withstanding, I would never breach a patient's confidentiality.

But obviously Gray and Addie had no qualms. "Ash do you know who this is?" Gray asked.

Ash shook his head even as Gray was answering himself. "The best nurse ever."

I felt me cheeks warm under the compliment.

Addie hugged me again. "You'll never know how much you, Mark and a few others did for me during those few awful days. Do you still see him?"

"He's dating my friend," I said.

"Oh, I wish you would have brought them along," Addie said, smiling. It was a smile that looked at home on her. As if this were her default expression.

When I'd seen her at the hospital, she'd been sad and introspective.

Yes, I was pretty sure this was closer to her normal state than the woman I'd met at the ICU.

"Next time you'll bring them," Gray said, as if there would definitely be a next time.

"Callum and Ash know each other," I said. "Ash was kind enough to extend the invitation to me and the kids."

"Ash and I are partners," Gray said.

"And friends," Addie added, admonishing him with a smile to do a better job describing his relationship to his partner.

Gray nodded.

"Tell Mark we asked about him," Addie said. "And tell him we both make it a point to say those three words often."

I wasn't sure what words she was talking about, but I nodded. "I will. How are you?"

"Fine," Gray said. Once he was well enough to talk, they'd moved him out of ICU, but for the short time he'd been awake on my unit, I realized that Gray was a man of few words.

"Fine and getting better every day," Addie said, filling in the words for him. "He's back to work part time, but I have Ash keeping an eye on him and his personal assistant Missy. They make sure he takes breaks and eats properly."

Maybe Gray had the luxury of saying few words because he had Addie to make up the difference, I thought with a smile.

As if to prove my point, she said, "I warn him that if he doesn't behave for them, I'm going to come renovate his office so I can keep an eye on him myself. And if I renovate, he'll have to get new art." She mock whispered, "He really likes his office as is, so he toes the line."

"I don't think I had this many people hovering over me in the hospital," Gray said. It sounded serious, but I was pretty sure it was a joke.

I smiled. "It's nice to know that many people care about you."

I pulled the kids close. "Jeremy and Haley, this is Mr. and Mrs. Grayson."

"It's nice to meet you," Addie said to the kids. "Your mom is a very special lady."

"Why don't you two come with me? We'll go get some food and I'll show you where the best seats are," Ash said.

Callum and Gray were talking quietly, so I looked at Addie. "You look much better than when I saw you last. Thank you for the letter and for the note to my supervisor."

After Gray moved from ICU to another floor of the hospital, I'd thought I'd heard the last from Addie. But a couple weeks later, a letter arrived for me and one for my supervisor. "It was so nice of you to write about me. It wasn't necessary."

"Oh, it was. I love sending *nice notes* to people who've helped me. So many people are quick to complain. I like to think my *nice notes* balance the scales. But Alice, it wasn't nearly enough. That was the least I could do. I mean it, the very least. You and Mark... Well, you two and a host of others were there for me during one of the lowest times in my life. You were..."

She teared up, which was all it took to make me tear up, too.

"Hey, it's my job," I said.

She shook her head. "No. You went way beyond your job description with us. Thank you for that."

"Gray needed you more than any medicine or medical procedure. He needed *you*." As I said the words, I realized I'd never needed Alan that way, and I was pretty sure he hadn't needed me either.

Maybe that's where our troubles began.

"And I needed him," Addie said, as if to prove my point.

She looked at him with such naked emotion I could almost see their love as a separate and physical entity.

Addie and I chatted. I'd known her as Gray's wife in the hospital. I found out she worked at a local furniture and design store, Harbor House. "I've been in there. I just bought a new place a while back and needed some furniture. I didn't know you worked there or I'd have asked for you."

"Next time, definitely ask for me," she said.

"Mom," Haley called.

"Pardon me," I said. I walked down the steps to where the kids were seated. "What's up?"

"Can me and Jeremy go down to see the players when they come back onto the ice after half time?"

Jeremy scoffed, reminding both of us half time was the wrong term.

"Intermission or whatever," Haley said. "That guy Ash said he'd take us down."

"Sure," I said. "Just check in with me before you go."

"Thanks, Mom," Haley said.

Jeremy just glared at me.

I was pretty sure he was thrilled to not only be at the game, but to be in a box. But he wasn't thrilled that I was dating. He seemed to be somewhere between those two contrasting emotions.

He hadn't threatened to runaway again, so maybe this was progress.

I didn't blame him, but I wasn't going to abide with him taking out his annoyance on anyone else.

"Be polite," I said as I patted his shoulder.

He pulled away.

I sighed.

I walked up the couple stairs to the box's main floor.

Callum looked at the back of the kids' head and then back at me with concern. "Maybe this wasn't such a great idea."

"It was very nice of you to include the kids. It's just going to take Jeremy some time."

"I get that he's not thrilled about me, but I hate that he's mad at you."

I tried to laugh it off. "I'm a mother. He spends a great deal of time being annoyed with me. Sometimes I deserve it and sometimes he's just a kid being a kid. Change is hard. And scary."

"Not just for him," Callum said.

Maybe he'd have said more, but Ash came over at that moment.

"So you met through work?" I asked. They seemed to have more than a purely business relationship.

"We met because Steele, Inc. sponsors things for the hospital on occasion," Ash said.

"By *sponsors*, he's being modest. They made a generous donation to our—"

"Shh," Ash said, shushing Callum.

"Shh?" Callum asked with a grin. "Did you really just shush me in front of my date?"

"Yes, I do believe that I shushed you. All you need to say is my company believes in being an active part of the community. And after Gray was sick, we redoubled our commitment to the hospital. You guys took wonderful care of him."

Ash looked at me as he said those words.

"They were easy to work with," I said.

"Addie is the soul of easiness, so I buy that she wasn't hard to work with. But I work with Gray every day. *Easy* doesn't quite work as a description." Ash was laughing at his own joke as he went with Callum and the kids.

"He seems nice," I said to Addie.

"He's the best. I keep threatening to set him up with some-one. He keeps telling me that I shouldn't wish him on my worst enemy. He does have a lousy track record with women."

Addie introduced me to some of the other people in the box. There were a lot of names I recognized. They were definitely not the kind of crowd I was used to socializing with. I was pretty sure that Olivia would fit right in with Erie's hierarchy.

She never said much about her family, but even before I met Hilary, I'd have guessed she came from some kind of money and power.

If she weren't dating Mark, I'd be tempted to have Addie set Olivia up with Ash.

As I watched the tall blond schmooze every woman in the box, from the oldest down to Haley, I decided that it was a good thing Olivia was seeing someone. That last thing she needed was a man who flitted from woman to woman like some sort of butterfly.

I was pretty sure Ash wouldn't like being called a butterfly, but I was equally pretty sure it was an accurate analogy.

As the evening wore on, I decided that if I had to see some-thing sporty, a box was definitely the way to go. I spent more time visiting with Addie and mingling than watching the game. Shooter, the team mascot, came up to the box. By then a little boy who had to be around three, Wills, and his baby brother, Joey had joined my kids. And it turned out both boys loved Jeremy.

I was sure Jeremy would deny it, but he was enjoying the boys. He held Wills' hand while Haley took Joey, up to meet the mascot.

"My boys are in heaven," said JoAnn, Addie's friend.

"My kids have a lot of practice with their little sister," I said.

"You should have brought her too," Addie offered.

"She's not mine, but I adore her, too," I finally said.

Neither woman pried.

There were so many ways to build a family these days, most people wouldn't.

After the hockey game, we went back to my house. Callum looked as if he were uncertain what to do.

"Come in," I offered. "The kids are heading up to bed."

"Sure," he said.

We all went in and got unbundled. Haley said, "Thank you, Mr. Callum. Ya know, that's a funny name."

"Haley," I admonished.

Callum didn't seem to be upset. "It is a funny name here in the US. It was my great-grandfather's name. My mom's father's father. That Callum came here from Scotland. The name's not so funny there. Mom gave me his kilt."

"Kilt?" Haley asked.

"A long time ago, guys in Scotland wore them instead of pants. They still do sometimes." Callum said.

"They're like skirts," I added, grinning as I said the word.

Callum mock glowered. "Hey, girls wear skirts. Men wear kilts."

"*Women* wear skirts," I corrected. "And so do men, they just give them a different name in order to feel good about the fact they're wearing a skirt," I teased.

Callum laughed and looked back at my daughter. "My name doesn't sound the least bit weird in Scotland. It's on the popular baby name list."

"But you're not a baby," Haley said innocently.

Jeremy was silent as we bantered back and forth. One mere *skirt* wasn't going to coax him out of his funk.

"It's time for bed, guys. I want to thank you though for being so nice to Wills and Joey," I said.

"They were cute, but not as cute as Bitty," Haley said.

"Yeah, we should have taken Bitty. She likes hockey. She probably missed us," Jeremy said.

"I'm sorry. I should have thought—" Callum started.

"No, Callum, please don't apologize. Jeremy should be the one saying he's sorry." I gave him a look that told him exactly what I expected.

"For what?" he protested.

"For being rude," I informed him.

"Yeah, I'm so sorry for being rude to your *boyfriend*," he said with just the right amount of ten-year-old sarcasm.

"Jeremy."

"Sorry, Mr. Callum," he mumbled then thumped up the stairs.

Haley looked uncertain. She glanced back at her brother, then turned to Callum. "Thanks for taking us to hockey. It was fun sitting in the box. Night, Mom." She hugged me then followed after Jeremy.

"I'm so sorry," I said.

"Don't be. He's a kid, trying to figure things out. I remember being totally unable to figure out why the adults in my life did the things they did."

"Thanks for being so understanding. Sometimes I think he blames me for his father leaving."

"Maybe he does. But maybe that's because you're safe to blame. I don't know the specifics and I'm not prying, but sometimes it's easier to be mad at the person who stays than to be mad at the person who left. Maybe he can be mad at you because he trusts you not to leave. He trusts you to always love him, even if he is sometimes a bit of a pill."

"You are a very nice man, Callum."

Alan had never tried to understand the kids, and though I tried it was nice to have someone else making an effort.

Sometimes it felt as if things had settled down into a new normal and then something changed again.

Jeremy really wasn't coping with any changes very well. Intellectually I knew that it made sense, but as a mother who wanted her kids to show the world their best possible self, it was hard to see him act like a pain.

"I should probably go," Callum said.

"Or you could stay for a while, if you like."

"We could watch an episode of Battlestar Gallactica together ... in the same room," he said.

Watching a show cuddled up to Callum rather than simply texting back and forth as we watched from our own homes would be novel.

"We definitely could. Or maybe ..." I leaned forward and kissed him. Partly because he was a nice guy.

Partly because he was trying to cut my son some slack.

And partly because I'd couldn't help think about our kiss on our date. I knew I wanted to repeat it.

But there was no repeating it. This kiss was even better. There was a hint of introduction, but there was more than that. There was a hunger. Not just mine. Not just his. *Ours.*

I lost myself in that kiss. I'm not sure how long we kissed, but I knew we stopped too soon.

"I would love more than this, but the kids ..." I said, feeling breathless.

"I understand."

Maybe it wasn't everything I wanted, but kissing Callum was definitely sweet. It was definitely on my plus-side for the day.

I leaned forward and lost myself again.

Chapter Twenty

Olivia

On the plus side: Life is full of surprises.

$\mathcal{I}$ was nervous about taking Bitty over to Mark's house. His father could be unpredictable according to Mark. And while his dad had been nice to me, I wasn't sure how he'd feel about my daughter.

I never imagined feeling so strongly about anyone before I had Bitty. But I knew with utter certainty that I would do anything to keep her from being hurt. And I knew that I couldn't.

That in and of itself was enough to make me a bit crazy.

But I didn't need to worry. It was love at first sight for Bitty and Mark's dad.

Really.

Watching Tyler West with Bitty was amazing. He held her and sang a version of *A Farmer in the Dell* with a rusty voice.

Bitty sat on his lap and helped with all the animal sounds. When Mr. West told her that pigs said *oink oink,* she insisted they said *moo.* And so he switched the sound in the song.

"What is that all about?" Mark whispered, glancing back at his father.

"I think your father likes kids."

"Not that I've ever noticed." Mark sounded mystified.

"Have you had a lot of kids around here?" I asked.

"No."

"Well, there you go. Maybe you missed it because of a lack of observation opportunities."

He was quiet as he dumped potatoes in a bowl, then said, "You know, I remember when I was little. I don't know how old. But Dad took me sled riding down the big hill at the back pasture. We came in and he made my hot chocolate, then we went out to do chores. I'd forgotten about the sled riding."

"Maybe so had he. Maybe Bitty is reminding him about a time when you were little and things were simple."

"Simple?" Mark asked.

I nodded. "Even if things are hard, everything is simpler when you're a kid. Children rarely worry about what happens next. They live in the *now*. They're happy. They're sad. They're hungry or tired, or they're having fun playing. They don't second-guess themselves and worry about what comes next."

I glanced back at my daughter and Mark's father. "Right now, Bitty is happy. She has someone who's willingly giving her a hundred percent of their attention and when you're a one-year-old, that's all that matters."

Mark looked back at Bitty and his dad. "Sometimes it's hard to remember a time we liked each other. He was so angry when I left and he's angry now that I'm home."

"Have you talked to him?" I asked softly.

"I talk to him every day."

"No, I mean really talked? You see, I met this man in a waiting room. I was nervous and he was kind. He listened and that act, just listening when I needed someone, made me feel better. Maybe you should talk to your dad. More than that, maybe you should really listen. Just because he was mad when you left doesn't mean he was mad the whole time you were gone. And just because he's mad now ... he might not be mad at you at all."

"Who would he be mad at?" Mark asked.

"Himself. If his drinking brought the farm to the brink of being sold I could see that making him mad. Or maybe he's frustrated at time itself, because it's beginning to weigh on him and keeps him from doing what he wants. I don't know him, but I can sit here and guess at all kinds of reasons. But that's just it, I'm just guessing. You won't know what's what until you ask him."

"You've made some good points. Listening is a big part of being a chaplain. I think it's easier to use that skill on strangers than on family."

I laughed. "It's always easy to think about other people's relationships. My mother has never even met Bitty. And try as I might, I can't understand how having a granddaughter doesn't mean anything to her." I didn't add, that I wasn't sure how having a daughter meant so little to her as well. She hated that I wouldn't conform to her wishes and be the daughter she wanted.

"Come to think about it, we both walked away from the lives our parents wanted for us," I said.

"But as you pointed out, here I am, a farmer."

I nodded. "Yes. But I will never be the daughter my mother wanted."

"Was she the mother you wanted?" he asked.

"I don't know. I love her. But I've never understood her any more than she understood me. That being said, there are things I can admire about her. She's strong. My father is not an easy man. And he's cheated on her. I had a friend in ninth grade point my father's mistress out to me. I caught him out with one of his ladies when I was a senior. He made up a lie, but he knew I didn't believe him. If I knew he had other women, my mother has to know. When I left, I asked her how she could stay with him. She told me it wasn't up to me, or anyone else, to judge her marriage."

I sighed. "You said something about trying to live by that nonjudgmental rule. Maybe I should have practiced what you preach. For a long time, I thought the fact that she stayed made her weak, but I've wondered since if staying made her strong?" I shook my head. "She was right. It wasn't my place to judge her."

But she'd judged me and found me lacking.

"So what you're saying is, we both need to figure out our relationships with our parents."

"Maybe. If we do, it might help us not make the same mistakes ourselves. I know that the relationship I have with my mother isn't the relationship I want Bitty to have with me."

Mark leaned over and kissed me. "You are an amazing woman."

"I am a woman who needs to get her act together. Alan was a mistake. I can't afford to make mistakes like that now that I have a daughter to think of." I was warning him and myself.

Falling in love with someone like Mark would be easy. But I needed to take my time and be sure. I couldn't risk screwing up Bitty's life. And though they weren't my kids, I had to think about Haley and Jeremy, too. And Alice.

When you're part of a family, you can't just think about yourself—about your wants and needs—because everything you do impacts the entire family.

Maybe that's why I called it an early evening. I used Bitty as an excuse, but was honest enough with myself to confess that I'd like nothing more than to stay at Mark's. I could picture us in that funky old country kitchen making dinner together, or sitting on the couch in the living room in front of the fireplace, watching Bitty play.

And the fact that it was so easy to imagine us there scared me.

I'd fallen head over heels with Alan. I no longer said I'd fallen in love, because I wasn't sure that was accurate. I'd fallen in love with the idea of love and Alan happened to be there.

I thought that was closer to the truth.

I hated to think I was looking for a father figure. I'd had a psychology class and it did seem plausible. My father was a letch. I'd never been able to look up to him. But Alan? He seemed to focus on me, and me alone. It was hard to imagine him cheating with someone else.

And in the end, he hadn't cheated on me, but rather used me to cheat on Alice.

No matter how many times she assured me it wasn't my fault, part of me still felt guilty.

I wasn't sure I'd ever shake that small part and frankly, I wasn't sure I should try. Maybe hanging onto that small bit of guilt would serve as a reminder to be careful in the future. Not to let myself get in that situation again.

Bitty was quiet in the back of the car as we drove back into the city. I was pretty sure she'd fallen asleep. If I were careful and quiet when I got home, I might be able to get her up to bed without waking her.

I'd go over and talk to Alice. I wanted to hear how her night with Callum and the kids went, and I wanted to have her play the voice of reason about me and Mark.

I knew she liked him and that was a huge plus in his favor.

But I suspected she'd agree with me ... slow and steady. That was the way to proceed.

Route 8 was dark. There were occasional streetlights, but most of the light came from homes. Sometimes just one window was glowing. Sometimes a whole house was alight.

All those families. Older couples, young families. Teenagers talking to their friends on the phone—no, I'd just dated myself—they'd be texting their friends. Couples falling in love.

I sighed.

But thoughts of couples and love kept intruding as I drove home.

I managed to get Bitty tucked in to bed without waking her and was about to knock lightly on Alice's door when I heard the sound of shouting.

Loud, angry voices.

I knocked then and didn't wait for a response as I pushed the door open and saw Jeremy. He was obviously the source of the screaming. He was standing, fists clenched at his side yelling at Alice and Callum.

I saw Callum stand up, his face red with anger. His hands were clenched as well. Softly, he said, "You should apologize to your mother."

"You're not my father. You can't tell me what to do," Jeremy screamed as he turned and ran up the stairs.

Callum stood there, frozen for a moment, then I watched all the color drain from his face. Without another word, he turned and walked out of Alice's house.

I didn't know what to say. What to do. "I'm sorry, Alice. I would never have just barged in, but I heard the screaming and..."

She shook her head. "No, I would have done the same thing."

"What was that?" I asked, sitting by her.

"Jeremy walked down and caught Callum and me kissing. I should go check on him, but I need a minute." She shook her head. "He'll probably think that makes me a bad mother, too."

"He said that?" I asked.

"Yes. Jeremy blames me for Alan leaving. He says I wanted to date other guys, that's the only reason. He knows that you dated Alan. I mean, he knows Bitty is his sister, but I don't think he's old enough to really understand what that means. And while

I may not be the best mother, I'm a good enough one not to poison him against his father by explaining."

"Alice, you're a very good mother," I said as I patted her hand.

She shook her head. "No. This all started because I needed that coffee in the morning after work. If I hadn't been selfish and had just headed home and never met Callum…"

"Oh, Alice." I had never been someone who had the appropriate emotions at the appropriate time, according to my mother. This was one of those times. I started laughing. "Seriously, if you're selfish then…" I couldn't even think of anything to say.

I shook my head and hugged her. "You are the most generous woman I've ever met. I'm pretty sure if I called Mark and asked him, he'd agree with me, not you. Taking a couple minutes for a coffee after a long night's work, that makes sense. You work in a high stress job."

She still looked a bit shaky. "Did you knock for something?"

Telling her that I thought I was falling for Mark and wanted her to talk me down—slow me down—didn't seem appropriate, so I just shook my head. "I came to let you know we were home."

"Did you have a nice time?" she asked.

I nodded. "A very nice time."

Maybe too nice a time?

"I should go up and see Jeremy now. And make sure Haley slept through that."

"No problem. I'll be next door if you need me."

She said something so softly I couldn't make it out. "What?"

"I said this isn't the life I had planned. I planned a perfect life. A nice house, a husband and kids. And now?"

I snorted. "Perfect is overrated. Neither of us planned to be here, but here is pretty good. Ten-year-old meltdown excluded."

She smiled. "Maybe you're right."

I went next door determined to remember my sage words to Alice. *Perfect is overrated. Here is pretty good.*

Maybe our lives weren't perfect, but if they were imperfect, they were perfectly so.

Perfectly imperfect. That was my plus-side tonight.

I smiled and put away worries of Mark for the night.

Chapter Twenty-One

Alice

On the plus side: Sometimes people can surprise you.

I'd barely finished my first cup of coffee the next morning when Alan showed up at my front door.

"Yes?" I asked, not inviting him inside.

He looked a bit ragged. "I came to see the kids."

"They're still sleeping." I waited for him to turn around and leave. I wasn't asking much out of life today, but I really, really wanted to finish my coffee before I had to deal with more kid drama.

"Are you going to invite me in?"

I almost groaned. Alan drama was even worse than kid drama. "I don't think so. If you want to see the kids I can text you when they get up."

"Alice. I'd like to think we could be adults."

Really? I wanted to shout, *really, Alan*? But I bit my tongue and said, "I would too, Alan, but I don't see that happening."

"What do you mean?" he asked, looking genuinely puzzled.

"Why on earth are you discussing my dating with the kids?" I snapped.

"Because I care—"

This time I couldn't hold back my snort. "If you cared about me, you'd want me to be happy."

"I do," he said.

"Then let me be. Stop poisoning our kids against my dates."

He frowned. "Dates?"

"Alan, you gave up the right to say anything about my personal life."

He sighed. "If I say I'm sorry and that I've felt bad about saying anything to Jeremy, could I come in?"

"Only if you swear you're going to be on your best behavior."

He nodded.

I moved aside and let him in.

"Would I be pushing my luck if I asked for a cup of coffee?" he asked as he trailed me into the kitchen.

"Fine." It wasn't very gracious, but to be honest, I was still annoyed about his comments to Jeremy. I really tried to get along with Alan. But it would be easier if he didn't seem to go out of his way to make things more difficult.

He sat down at the table and took a long sip of his coffee. "No one can make coffee like you do."

He'd said that to me the first time right after we married.

I remembered how happy we'd been then, but somewhere along the line we'd stopped being happy and started to be complacent. I could blame a lot of things on him but complacency was on both of us. "Alan, is there anyway we can find a way to…"

Not be friends. I might want to get along with him, but friends wasn't in the picture. But maybe… "Allies? Co-parents? I need your help. If it was just two of us ending a marriage, I'd say let's just walk away and get on with our own lives. But we have our kids. And you and Olivia have Bitty. That means we all will be connected for the rest of our lives. School functions. Graduations. College. Marriages. Grandkids."

Grandkids? I could hardly imagine Jeremy or Haley having children of their own.

"Think about it. We are tied for the rest of our lives. I'd like to find a way to be at all the big life events and not have drama or tension. I don't expect you to be best friends with someone I date, but I need you to be polite. And I swear I'll be polite to people you date."

I paused a moment and ventured a joke. "We already know I like the people you date."

Alan stopped short a moment, and then he chuckled. "You always had an weird and inappropriate sense of humor."

I laughed as well. "So that gives us a foundation to start to build a new relationship on. You like my coffee and even when you don't want to, you find me amusing."

"And you truly are one of the best parents I've ever met. I don't say it to you and Olivia often enough, but I do notice how good you both are."

"You were always a good father." I didn't add that the last year he'd been less so.

But then, I didn't need to.

"I know I haven't been this last year. And I'm sorry. Sorry for all of it. You didn't deserve my cheating. And Olivia didn't deserve my lies. I don't know how it happened. I screwed up. I think I wasn't as active in the kids' lives because I'm embarrassed by how much I messed things up, not just for me, you and Olivia, but for them."

Finally, after more than a year, here was the man I remembered. It made things easier. "So let's start again. I think that's one of life's biggest gifts…the do-over. Let's agree that we'll always put the kids first. I don't even have to ask Olivia to know she's onboard."

"And putting the kids first means letting Jeremy see I'm okay with your guy."

"And Olivia's."

He slowly nodded. "So, why don't I wait around for them to wake up and take all three kids for the day. You and Olivia can come pick them up tomorrow at lunch. I'll order pizza. And your dates are welcome."

"Really?"

He nodded. "It's time I stopped being an asshole."

I choked and then started laughing. Olivia knocked on the door and came in, Bitty racing ahead of her. "Da," the baby shouted and Alan picked her up.

"What's going on?" Olivia asked.

I was still laughing too hard to answer, so Alan said, "Alice and I agreed I've been an," he covered Bitty's ears with his hands and whispered, "ass. I'm agreeing to mend my ways. Or at least acknowledge my mistakes and try to do better."

"Just what's in the coffee this morning?" Olivia asked, helping herself to a mug.

I laughed . . . and so did Alan.

"I still don't understand your friendship," he said. Before either of us could retort, he held up a hand and added, "But it's good for the kids and that's what matters."

I knew we were bound to have problems in the future, but suddenly the future looked brighter.

That was my plus-side for the day.

When the kids woke up, they were excited to spend the day with Alan. As they got ready, I texted Callum. *I have an unexpected free afternoon. If you're free, I'd like to spend it with you.*

He texted back one word, *Yes.*

And that was another plus-side.

Chapter Twenty-Two

Olivia

On the plus side: Unexpected Moments

"Really what did you put in Alan's coffee?" I asked Alice again. It was time someone told him to grow up. The three of us are connected through our kids. We're stuck with each other for the rest of our lives. All three of us need to remember that what matters the most is the kids. I could blame everything on Alan, but it's hard to find a way to get along with someone you're so angry at. Today, I finally got past the anger and was willing to say the words. And he was finally able to hear them.

Alice was not a hugger, well, other than the kids and knowing that, I didn't press the issue most of the time with her. But this once, I couldn't help myself. I hugged her long and hard. "Thank you."

"We're family. Alan too. The kids are at the center and all the adults—you, me, Alan, and any other significant others any of us someday have—have to put them first. They have to be the priority."

We spent the morning together, cleaning our respective houses and then had lunch together sans kids.

Sometimes I forgot that Alice was more than just family, she was a friend. Moments like this were rare, but treasured.

"I'm going to meet Callum this afternoon," she said. "I was afraid that after last night, he was going to say no."

"I've seen how he looks at you," I said. "He's not going to say no."

She didn't respond to my statement. I don't think Alice truly saw how amazing she was, but everyone else did. Maybe all her years as a nurse had made her so kind and empathetic. But I suspected it was the other way around. Her kindness and empathy had led her to nursing. I know that if I were sick, I'd want her taking care of me.

"Are you going to call Mark?" she asked instead.

I shrugged. "I don't know. It feels cheeky to just call him up and say the kids are gone, what are you up to?"

"Cheeky? Sometimes, Olivia, you seem much older than I know you are." She laughed. "Call him. I've seen him when he's with you or even just talking about you. He won't mind."

And so, I called him to see if he had time to get together. He asked if I'd mind coming out to the farm.

Mind? No, I didn't mind at all. I already loved the farm.

He told me to meet him in the back barn.

It was one of those March days that practically shouted that spring's just around the corner. The sky was robin egg blue. Not one cloud marred that blueness. I knew in the next month or so daffodils and crocuses would start popping up.

As I got farther into the county, I occasionally saw cows out in their pastures. Some looked huge and though I wasn't a farmer, I suspect soon they'd all be calving.

Yes, it was a day that spoke of new beginnings.

And I realized that I wanted any new beginning for myself to include Mark.

Maybe it was too soon to think about things like that, but maybe when you found the right person there was no such thing as *too soon.*

I realized that if we did have a future together, there were challenges. His dad. Alan.

Those were incidental.

Alice would be the biggest hurdle if Mark and I went any further than just dating.

I knew he wouldn't be able to move into our flat, and I knew that me moving here someday would mean leaving Alice, Haley, and Jeremy.

How could I choose between the people I love?

Love.

It hit me then. It hit me so hard I pulled over the side of the road down in the hollow by a swamp.

I love Mark.

I thought I'd loved Alan, but that felt like a lifetime ago. And those feelings I'd had for Alan seemed pale and lacking when I compared them to what I felt for Mark.

I wasn't going to rush anything.

I wasn't going to tell Mark yet. No, I wanted to savor this feeling for a while.

It was strong and it wasn't going anywhere.

I couldn't seem to stop smiling as I continued driving to the farm. I was thankful no cops pulled me over because they'd be convinced that I was drunk because I'm sure I looked that goofy.

I pulled into the drive and drove all the way down to the back barn. I slipped on my Wellingtons.

The air out here smelled like life. Fresh with an undercurrent of dirt.

I smiled even more broadly at the thought. I tried to rein my expression in before I went into the barn, but I wasn't sure I was successful.

"Mark?" I called.

"Over here."

I walked to a well-lit corner of the barn that he used as a workshop. And when I saw his project I felt tears fill my eyes even as I continued to smile.

"I wanted to give Bitty and Haley something to do out here this summer," he said as if it was a given I'd be coming out here this summer with the kids. "I have an old clubhouse in the back. I looked at it, and really all it needs is a new roof. I thought they all might want to *help* me fix that up."

I moved closer to the playhouse and inside was a smaller playhouse.

"I bought a Barbie. I know, I'm so manly," he laughed and continued, "but I wanted to be sure the dollhouse would work. It folds up flat against the wall and—"

He didn't get any further because I catapulted myself into his arms and kissed him.

"What was that for?" he asked when we finally broke apart.

"That was because I love you."

There they were. The words I thought I'd hold onto and savor for a while. Finally, I stopped smiling, wondering if I'd ruined everything with my premature declaration. "Listen, you don't have to say anything back. We've only known each other five months and only had a handful of dates. I wasn't going to say anything, but when I saw you thinking about not just my daughter, but the other kids, I swear, I was about to burst and it just exploded on its own. You don't have to …"

My sentence faded because Mark had placed a finger over my lips and said, "Shh." He kissed me again. "I love you, too."

Chapter Twenty-Three

Alice

On the plus side: Family.

I sat next to Callum on his couch as we watched another episode of Battlestar Gallactica. There was an assortment of Chinese takeout boxes on the coffee table and a open bottle of wine next to our glasses.

As the credits ended, he leaned forward and kissed my neck. His breath tickled. But I didn't laugh. I felt flushed and happy.

"The kids are with Alan all night?" he asked, his words, like his breath, brushing my neck and making me feel even warmer.

"Yes," I managed.

"Then would you like to stay the night?" he asked.

And as I looked at Callum, I didn't think or analyze, I merely answered his question. "Yes."

I woke up the next morning and looked at Callum.

He was still sleeping, but a light smile played on his lips.

I was pretty sure if I looked in the mirror, I'd see my expression echoing his.

He woke up with a start and his smile broadened when he saw me. "Hello," he said.

"Hello yourself. Sorry I woke you."

"You didn't," he said.

"Oh, I did. I was staring at you. When my kids were younger, they woke me up that way all the time."

"They stared you awake?" he asked with a laugh.

"Yes. I never knew how effective it was until this morning."

"Why were you staring at me?"

"I was thinking. I don't have to pick the kids up at Alan's until lunch, so that means we have time to ..." I gave him my best come-hither look. I'm not sure how good it was, but it was good enough for him to get the message and pull me back under the covers.

I love you, I wanted to cry out, but I didn't. Not yet. The feeling was too new and frankly, too intense.

But as we made love, the words were a part of the cadence.

Every touch, every kiss, every look. They were all my way of telling him that I loved him.

A few days later, Callum met me for coffee.

"More problems with Jeremy?" he asked.

I took a sip of my coffee and shook my head. "I'm worried about one of my nurses. She's said things in the past that made me concerned about her boyfriend, and ..." I didn't want to break my nurse, Sunny's confidence, but Callum was in HR. "She had to quit unexpectedly. Things escalated with her boyfriend. I let her use up her vacation as her two weeks notice and leave in good standing. I'll have to work a couple extra shifts to fill in for her, but I think it was okay to do it. And if it's not, I hope you'll figure out a way to make it okay. If she comes back to town, I want to offer her back her job. She was a great nurse and—"

He silenced me with a kiss. "As nurse manager you have the discretion to do that, so it's all good. But that's not going to stop you worrying about her."

"I'll confess, I'll worry less now that she's gone. There was something very wrong about her relationship. Her husband called and texted her non-stop. If she was late, she always let him know if she could, but I saw her expression a few times, Callum. I offered to help if I could."

"Sounds like by leaving, she helped herself. She's lucky she had you in her corner."

"I don't know. It doesn't feel like I did enough," I said.

"Sometimes just listening and letting someone know you support them without judging them is enough."

That's what he was doing for me. I reached over and took his hand in mine. "Thank you."

"You're welcome."

"I was making up my plusses and minuses today."

"Which won?" he asked.

"Well, it was close, because I was worried about Sunny, but then you came along and said just the right thing, so you're the plus that put me over the finish line."

"I always hope I stay on your plus side."

To be honest, I couldn't imagine Callum anywhere but on the plus side.

Chapter Twenty-Four

Alice

On the minus side: Everything changes.
On the plus side: Everything changes.

The next month sped by. Callum was a bit more comfortable with my kids and Haley seemed to accept he was part of our lives.

Jeremy was still displaying some very obvious Jekyll and Hyde tendencies. One moment he seemed to accept Callum as part of our new lives, then next... not so much.

It didn't help matters that Olivia spent so much time at the farm with Mark. It was another change in their lives and neither of the kids was sure how they felt.

To be honest, I wasn't sure how I felt.

I was thrilled that Olivia seemed so genuinely happy. Mark was one of the good ones, so I was thrilled about that as well. But I missed having Olivia next door all the time. It made me feel selfish, but it also made me more understanding when I dealt with the kids. Especially when I dealt with Jeremy's mood swings.

It seemed every time I had a handle on things, the world shifted and there was a new status quo to get used to.

Maybe that's what life was…a continuous shifting of circumstances.

Maybe our job was to find the plus side in each new phase.

With that in mind, as Bitty played with Duplos and I started the corned beef and cabbage for St. Patrick's Day dinner, I started my list.

On the plus side: I'd heard from Sunny and she was okay.

On the plus side: Callum was amazing.

On the plus side: Haley liked him most of the time, and Jeremy seemed to like him more than he didn't like him.

On the plus side: Alan was still trying.

On the minus side: Olivia was gone more and more with Bits.

On the plus side: She seemed happier than I'd ever seen her.

On the plus side: Mark and Callum seemed to genuinely like each other.

On the minus side: It felt as if everything was in a state of flux again.

Bitty squealed, got up and ran to the front door. She had some inner radar that let her know when the kids were coming home. They'd gotten a ride with a friend this afternoon. I loved our unofficial carpool. All of us switched off when needs be. I enjoyed afternoons when I didn't have to face the afterschool chaos in the school parking lot.

"Mom, Mom, guess what?" Haley said, racing ahead of Jeremy. "I'm going to be a robin in the spring play. I've got a note for you on how to make a robin costume. You gotta do it right 'cause Amalie is the other robin and her mom is good at sewing. She made Amalie a dress for Christmas that was awesome and…"

Haley continued her breathless description of Amalie's dress, the costumes and her part in the play as Jeremy came in with Bitty on his hip. He seemed so old all of a sudden. So did Bitty. So did Haley. That sense of impending change swept over me again.

I realized I didn't want things to change. I'd built a good life for myself and the kids. And I wanted to revel in it as long as possible. I wanted to build memories that I could—

"What is that smell?" Jeremy asked, by way of a greeting.

"So, no *hi Mom*, or *how was your day, Mom?*" I teased as he wrinkled his nose.

"No," he said, shaking his head. "What did you do?"

He grinned in such a way that I knew this was another fart joke. It seems that farts are the height of comedy for boys. I smiled as I said, "It wasn't me."

He laughed which made Bitty laugh. She might not know what was funny, but she did know if Jeremy was laughing, it had to be good.

I said, "It's corned beef and cabbage for dinner."

"Maybe we should call Dad and see if he wants to come get us for dinner, Haley?" Jeremy said, teasing.

His little sister caught on and nodded, "And if he can't, maybe Olivia will feed us."

"Nah, if she's cooking, it will probably smell that way, too," Jeremy teased.

I laughed. "I don't think she's an option anyway. She's going to Mark's tonight," I said, as they grinned.

Jeremy nodded. "I bet she'd let us come, too," he said with a laugh.

I shrugged. "Well, that's too bad, because I have dessert."

"What kind of dessert?" Jeremy asked, ready to deal.

"Cake. And ice cream."

He sighed. "Looks like we'll have to eat dinner with plugged up noses, Haley."

They continued to tease me some about the smell of the cabbage. I agreed, cooked cabbage smelled, but it did taste amazing.

Olivia came in. "I finished," she said, then wrinkled her nose. "What on earth is that..."

"Stench?" Jeremy filled in. "Cabbage. Mom swears it'll taste good, but I figure it only tastes good because you have to plug your nose to eat it, so you can't really taste anything."

The doorbell rang. "Ha. I have reinforcements." I went and let in Callum. "No matter what, don't you agree with my son," I warned him.

"About?" he asked with a smile.

"Hey, Callum, watch out, Mom's trying to poison us," Jeremy called.

"Bits and I are leaving before we're forced to take sides," Olivia said.

I kissed the baby and told them to have fun as Callum aligned himself with the kids, despite my warning.

"Hey, Alice, what do you think about pizza tonight?" he teased.

"I think it's St. Patrick's Day and we're all eating an Irish meal."

Dinner was filled with more cabbage comments, but I noticed everyone managed to eat it. And the ribbing moved on to Callum, who mashed the potatoes, cabbage, and carrots all together. It looked disgusting.

"My grandfather ate it like this. He called it *hot lead*."

"I call it gross," said Haley.

"Yeah, me too," Jeremy agreed.

I was more polite and didn't voice my opinion, but my opinion was they were right.

"Try it," Callum challenged them.

Soon, there was mashing and more laughter.

The kids ran upstairs to start homework and Callum helped me start the dishes. "Happy St. Patrick's Day," he said as he kissed me.

"The kids are going to Alan's this weekend. I wondered if you'd like—"

My phone rang, interrupting my invitation. I pulled it from my back pocket and saw it was work. "I've got to take it."

Turned out the snow on top St. Patrick's Day made for a busy night at the hospital. We were shorthanded since Sunny left. "I'll be there as soon as I can."

My plans for a quiet evening with Callum and the kids disappeared. "I've got to go into work. I've got to call Olivia and see if she can come home early."

Callum shook his head. "Go ahead. I'll stay until Olivia gets home tonight."

"Are you sure?" Callum seemed to be more comfortable coming over to my house. And things had seemed good tonight with Jeremy, but just last week we'd had another blowup. "I can call Alan, too."

"I'm a grown man," Callum said. "I can handle two kids, especially ones who have to be in bed soon because tomorrow's a school day."

I laughed. "Yes, I guess if you're going to start watching kids, sleeping ones are the easiest."

He kissed me. "I'm really trying."

"I know." I'd met people who weren't comfortable with kids in the past, but Callum seemed to take it to a whole new level.

"Well, thank you. I don't think Olivia will be too late. The snow's really starting to come down and she doesn't like driving in it with the baby." I laughed. "I'm going to have to stop calling Bitty a baby. She's definitely a toddler now."

I texted Olivia, packed clothes for the morning, and changed into my scrubs. I called the kids down. "I got called into the hospital. Callum's going to stay with you until Olivia gets home."

"Great," Jeremy said.

I shot my son a look.

He sighed. "I'll behave."

I went to work hoping they did behave for Callum. I didn't want him to run to the hills. I really wanted us to make it work.

When I was with Alan, I thought I'd built a perfect marriage and family. I wasn't shooting for perfect any more. But I was pretty sure that Callum and I could have something very good.

I had never been so exhausted. I don't understand people. I mean I enjoy a cold beer as much as the next person, but drinking yourself silly...that I don't get. We'd had a plethora of alcohol poisonings and there were five car accidents, though I maintain if you are drinking and driving, that's not an accident.

Olivia had called and said the roads in the county were horrible. She'd talked to Callum and he said he'd spend the night. She apologized profusely. I called Callum to offer to send Alan over, but he'd assured me he could handle sleeping kids.

When my shift ended, I showered quickly and hurried home.

I was sure Callum could handle things, but I don't think he was as confident.

Despite being exhausted, I'll confess, I liked heading home and knowing Callum would be there waiting.

I was smiling as I unlocked the front door. My smile evaporated as I opened it.

"I hate you," I could hear Jeremy scream.

"Be that as it may, you may not ever hit your sister again. Ever." Callum's voice was low, but it carried as I hurried back into the kitchen. "Hitting is for cowards."

"You're not my father," Jeremy screamed. "You can't tell me what to do."

Callum was holding Haley who was crying on his shoulder.

"No, but I'm your mother," I said as I entered the room, "and you and I both know I shouldn't have to say it, but here goes. No hitting anyone, ever."

"I hate you, too," Jeremy screamed and ran out of the room.

I looked at Callum. "Go check on him. Me and Haley are fine. Right sweetie?"

Haley turned to me and nodded. There was a red mark on her cheek. I presumed it was where Jeremy hit her.

I ran over and kissed her and shot Callum a look of gratitude and hurried up the stairs after my son.

His door was shut.

I didn't bother knocking. I opened it and saw him sprawled on his bed, sobbing.

"Jeremy?" I said as I sat on the edge of the bed.

"I didn't mean to hit Haley. I came down and Callum was still here giving her another pancake and they were laughing. And then he looked at me and said he had pancakes for me, too. And then I said no and Haley said '*come on Jeremy, there're good.*' Then she said '*Daddy never makes us pancakes.*' And she took a bite."

"And?" I prompted softly.

"And I hit her. I said that Callum's not her dad, and that Dad could make pancakes if he wanted and they'd be better than stupid Callum's. And she was crying. And then Callum said, we never hit people. And I said, he wasn't my father and couldn't tell me what to do." He sobbed again. "I hate him. If you didn't date him, then Dad could come home and we could be a family again."

"Jeremy, your father and I are never getting back together. He doesn't love me, and I don't love him. It's hard enough to make a relationship work if you love each other. It's impossible if you don't."

"But I love you and I love him," Jeremy said.

"I know sweetie, I know. And that's why your dad will always be a part of our family, even if I'm not married to him."

"It wasn't Callum, was it?" he asked.

I shook my head. "I didn't meet Callum until your dad had moved out and we were divorced."

"Dad cheated on you with Olivia, didn't he? That's why Bitty's our sister."

Jeremy was only ten. Ten-year-olds shouldn't know about parents cheating. But I'd never lied to him. That didn't mean I had to tell him the whole truth.

The problem was, I couldn't think of a satisfactory explanation.

"It's okay, Mom. I know. And I know that Dad didn't tell Olivia about us. She didn't know about us."

"Honey, your dad made a mistake. That doesn't mean…" I didn't know what that didn't mean. "He's not perfect. Neither am I. And neither are you, or Haley, or Callum. We're all people who do dumb things and make mistakes. We can try to be perfect, but we'll never be that. So maybe it's better to just try and do our best."

"Hitting Haley wasn't my best," he said.

I shook my head and smoothed his hair. "No."

"And being mad at Callum wasn't it either. He didn't do anything. I was just so mad when I woke up and saw him in the kitchen. I thought he stayed with you all night, but he said Olivia couldn't come home 'cause of the snow and you worked. Then Haley said he was making pancakes and Dad never did that."

"That's not quite true," I said.

"What?"

"Your dad made pancakes once when you were very little. They were like hockey pucks. I mean, they were awful. But you took one, because he made it for you, and you gnawed on it and tried to eat it. Then your dad tried one and realized how bad they were. But your dad does make great scrambled eggs."

"Even I can make scrambled eggs," Jeremy scoffed.

"Don't tell your Dad," I said. "His eggs are his one point of cooking pride."

And then we both laughed. And Jeremy hugged me and I hugged him back. "I love you," I said.

"I know. And even if you love a thousand other people, you'll always love me."

"Even if I loved a million other people."

He said, "And I guess Callum's not so bad."

"I kinda like him," I admitted.

"I do, too. Sometimes," he qualified.

"He'll never take the place of your father, Jeremy. He cares about you though."

"Yeah. I guess I need to go say I'm sorry."

"That sounds like a good idea."

I went down with him as he made his apologies. I couldn't read Callum's mood as I got the kids ready and out the door.

Our foot of snow might have made for a school snow-day in other cities. But this was Erie. A foot of snow barely slowed the city down.

After the kids left, I went back into the kitchen and poured myself another cup of coffee. "Callum, I'm so sorry. I didn't think you'd be here all night, and then having to deal with the kids—"

"It was the best thing that ever happened to me," he said.

"You're weird," I told him with a smile. "I've dealt with their fights before. They're awful."

"Don't you see? I did deal with it."

"I never had any doubt that you could."

"I did," he said softly. "Listen, I told you that it was just my mom and me for as long as I can remember. That's not quite true. I remember bits of when my father was with us. I remember him hitting my mother. The last time I saw him, I ran in the room and told him not to touch her. He hit me then. Hit me so hard I ended up smacking up against the wall. I had a concussion. My mom kicked him out then."

"Callum, I'm so sorry." I couldn't imagine letting anyone hit me or my kids. I thought about Sunny and her ex. I'd dealt with abuse in the hospital, but Sunny and Callum were the first times I'd known people personally who'd dealt with it.

I realized there was a good chance I knew more people who, like Callum, had dealt with it but didn't talk about it.

I reached over and held his hand. "I am so sorry."

Callum said, "I've read studies that say that children who were abused are more prone to becoming abusers. I never wanted to take the chance..."

I heard what he wasn't saying. "So you never dated women with children."

He nodded. "I swore I'd never have kids and take the chance that I might be like my father. But Alice, I fell for you and your kids are part of the package deal. I know that. I haven't been around on Tuesday and Thursday nights because I'm taking a child development class. And Wednesday mornings, I'm taking a step-parenting class at the hospital. I don't want you to think that I'm just expecting us...you..." He gave up trying to explain and went on. "I just want to know how to cope with them. I figure if I know what to expect, I might not screw it up too bad. But then this morning..."

"Jeremy was mad. He thought you spent the night with me."

Callum nodded. "I saw when he came into the kitchen he wasn't happy to see me here. And he hit his sister. I was furious. I mean, absolutely furious. And I explained that hitting isn't acceptable ever. Alice, I was so angry but I coped with it. If you hadn't come home, I'd have sent him to his room to wait for you. I wouldn't have hit him. I know that."

I could see how worried he'd been. "I wish you'd have told me this was bothering you earlier. I'd have told you I would never let anyone hurt my kids. I don't think I ever knew how strong

I was until last year. I guarantee you that I'm strong enough to stop you if you ever lost control. But you won't. Do you know how I know that?"

"How?" he asked.

"You're strong, too. Much stronger than your father. Because you know that hurting someone, especially someone weaker than you, isn't a sign of strength, but rather of weakness. Your father was a weak, scared little man. You are not that. You could never be that."

"Alice," he said, his voice cracking.

"Callum, you are not your father and I am not my mother. We are Alice and Callum and we are two of the strongest people I've ever met."

"And we're even stronger together than we are apart," Callum said.

I nodded. "Exactly."

"I'm not perfect," he added.

"Neither am I. And that's good. I watched my mother move from place to place, from man to man. Always looking for something or someone to make her life better. I decided I wouldn't wait for that. I'd build a perfect life for myself. I thought I'd built one. A perfect husband. A perfect home. Perfect kids."

I laughed and added, "One out of three isn't bad."

He didn't say anything, or laugh, so I said, "I meant the kids were perfect. Not that they're perfect mind you. I'm not one of those my-kids-never-do-anything-wrong moms. But they're perfect for me. When I realized that, I realized that's what I need. *Perfect for me.* Maybe what's perfect for me will change with time. Maybe in the end, perfect is a fluid concept."

He was still silent, so I finished what I had to say. "Here's what I know. You are not perfect. But you are perfect for me."

"And I have known for a long time that you are perfect for me. And for the first time in my life, I believe that I am strong enough."

Finally, I felt like I could say the words that had been on the tip of my tongue for a long time. "I love you."

"I love you, too," he said.

Olivia walked in the door that was still open between our homes. "Man, what a crazy storm. But the plows came through and it wasn't such a bad drive home. Thanks for staying, Cal..."

She looked at the two of us. "What did I miss?"

I looked at Callum and we both started to laugh.

"What?" Olivia asked.

Callum and I hugged each other and kept laughing.

Perfect may be a fluid concept, but I knew I'd always remember this moment as being perfect.

Chapter Twenty-Five

Olivia

On the plus side: Everything.

"Me and haley talked," Jeremy announced as he stormed into the living room and glared at his mother and me.

"About?" Alice asked.

"About you guys and the guys and me, Haley, and Bitty," Jeremy said. "We say no."

"No to what?" Alice asked.

"We like Mark and we like Callum, but we ain't moving. So if you two are gonna get all kissy with 'em and marry 'em, then okay. I know I've been mean to Callum sometimes, but I'm done with that," he told his mother. "But don't kiss in front of us 'cause it's gross. But me and my sister decided we ain't moving so they'll have to move in here."

"Honey," Alice started, but that was obviously stumped by the right thing to say.

I felt so guilty. Mark and I had talked about just this problem. "Jeremy no matter where I live—"

"No," he said. "You don't get to tell me I'm just a kid and I have to do what the grownups say. 'Cause I know I'm a kid, but Bitty's my sister, Olivia. And if you move or we move, then

Bits won't be near us any more. And she needs me and Haley. Dad isn't around much and she needs someone too look out for her. That's what me and Haley do. We're gonna teach her to ride bikes and how to spit and watch more Star Wars with her, and maybe Star Trek and I was gonna ask for a telescope for my birthday so I could show Bits and Haley the stars. They're just girls, but they can do anything and that means they can be astronauts, too. And maybe we'll all three go to Mars someday. 'Cause I can't go and leave them behind. But..."

His heart was breaking.

"Mom, you and Dad broke up and I get that, he's a dork, but we love him 'cause he's our dad, but he was mean to you and Olivia. And we moved here. I was so mad for a long time, but then I liked it here. I like it. Not the house, but us. We're a family. I don't want that to change."

"Honey," Alice tried again.

"Nope. That's all me and Haley and Bitty have a say and we're not moving away from each other. So, you guys gotta figure it out."

He picked up Bitty, who was almost too big for him to carry and left the room for our side of the house, with Haley on his heels.

"So, what do we do now?" Alice asked me.

"I don't have a clue. But Mark and I have had discussions about this. He wants me to marry him, Alice. But taking Bitty away from all of you might break my heart."

"So what are we going to do?" Alice asked again.

We got the kids ready for Alan. He was taking them for the day.

When they all left, we sat in Alice's living room quietly for a few minutes. Finally I said, "I'm in love."

"I know. Anyone with eyes can see that," Alice said. "And I love Callum."

"Yes, you do. So what if we both take our relationships to the next step? I don't want to lose you all."

"Ditto."

"What if—" My phone rang, interrupting me.

I hummed the theme of Jaws and Alice asked, "Your mom?"

I nodded and answered the phone as I walked towards the kitchen. "Hi, Mom."

"Olivia, Hilary and I are taking a trip to New York next month," she said without preamble. "We'd love to have you join us."

"That sounds like fun, but I'm not sure I can get away, Mom."

"Oh, I'm sure *that woman* will keep the baby for a week. You watch her children a lot. She owes you."

I sighed. "She doesn't owe me a thing, Mom. I owe her more than you'll ever know."

"I don't know how you can say that. Why—"

"Mom, this is it. I'm done. I hope you keep in touch, and I'd love for you to come see me, but there are rules."

"Rules?"

"Rules." Remembering Alice's discussion with Alan gave me a blueprint. "You may not talk about Alice like that. And if you do talk about her, you need to use her name. *Alice.* Not *that woman.* She's family, Mom. Jeremy and Haley are too. They will be part of my life for the rest of my life."

"Olivia …"

"And you should know, there's a new man in my life. He's a local farmer and minister. I'd love to have you meet him, but same rules apply. My relationship with him isn't yours to judge, but simply to accept."

"Really? I feel as if you've always judged me for staying with your father. Do those rules swing both ways?"

"Mom…" What could I say? How could I justify myself? She was right. "I'm sorry. You're right. I have judged you. Your relationship with Dad is your own."

"He'd like a relationship with you. No matter what's happened between the two of us, he's always loved you and your absence hurts him," she said softly. "We've stayed away because we didn't think you were open to it."

I felt ashamed. I couldn't condone my father's affairs, but he was as much a part of my family as Alan. "Mom, I'm very sorry."

"He hasn't… Well, the two of us are better now. Stronger. But we've missed you."

"I'd love to have you two come visit. I'd like to have you meet everyone."

"I'll talk to your father and get back to you to make arrangements," she said back to her normal briskness.

"Mom, I am sorry and I look forward to your visit."

"Me, too," she said and then added, "I love you," right before she hung up.

I walked back into the living room feeling shell-shocked.

"What happened?" Alice asked.

"I just got called out by my mother," I said sinking onto the couch. "And while that might not be unusual, I have to say she was right. You stood up to Alan and pointed out that all of us were tied through the kids for the rest of our lives. We needed to find a way to get along. Well, it's the same with my father. I can't condone what he did, but it's not mine to judge."

"I think that for tonight, we should put away our worries about what comes next and simply revel in the fact that we've built a family… Alan included. And we've both found wonderful guys."

I nodded. "Can I tell you something?"

Alice nodded.

"I don't want our family to change," I said. "And if things keep going the way they are between me and Mark, and you and Callum, they're bound to change. For the first time in my life, I feel I've found my family and I'm right where I belong."

"Me, too," Alice said, her eyes welling up with tears.

"But I also feel like I've found the right guy...finally," I said. Alan might be part of our family, but he was never the right man for either of us."

"Yes," she said.

"I understand how Jeremy feels," I muttered. "Being a grownup sucks."

Alice lifted her glass. "I'll toast that sentiment."

We clinked glasses.

We didn't solve anything, but I felt more at peace than ever.

I wasn't sure if it was building a new bridge with my mother, or feeling as if we had Alan settled as an auxiliary part of our family, or if it was Mark, the kids, or Alice...

Suddenly I realized that I had a lot to be happy about.

And despite being on the cusp of a new change, I felt as if it was going to be a very good change.

Chapter Twenty-Six

Alice
May

On the plus side: Life changes, but change can be good.

Life changed once again.

But it was a good change.

Olivia was at Mark's house a lot, but she was very conscious about spending time in town with the kids. Mark was around too.

And Callum was at my house most days after work. We made dinner together. He helped the kids with homework as much as I did. We found a rhythm and it worked. We still met for our morning coffees on days I worked.

The kids would start summer vacation soon and our rhythm would change once again, but I was looking forward to having them around during the day.

I could picture trips to Presque Isle to go swimming, hikes at Asbury Woods, and spending time at the farm. They loved *helping* Mark, who was kind enough to never point out their help wasn't always... well, helpful.

"Good morning, Serena," I called out. I looked around for Callum.

Serena laughed as she handed me two coffees. "He's not here yet."

"Thanks. Have a wonderful day." I pushed a bill toward her and took the coffees to our table and started my list as I took my first sip.

On the plus side: Hot coffee in the morning.

On the plus side: It was a quiet, uneventful shift.

On the plus...

"You look happy," Callum said as he slipped into his chair.

I pushed his coffee toward him. "I am."

"Did the plusses win this morning?"

"Would I sound horribly sappy if I said they always do when you're around?" I laughed, knowing it did indeed sound sappy.

"Yeah, but I like it."

"How was your night?"

"Lonely. I helped Olivia get the kids settled before I went home."

"Thank you. I don't want you to feel as if you have to."

"Alice, I want to. You've told me time and time again that you and Olivia are family by choice. I get it. The kids are family... by choice. You see, I love you, so your family is my family. So all the kids, Olivia, Mark, and even Alan."

I couldn't help myself. I stood up, leaned over the table and kissed him.

He looked at me oddly. "I was going to ask you out on a formal date this week."

I laughed. "What is a formal date?"

"One where we get all dressed up and go to some fancy restaurant."

I hated getting dressed up, but if Callum wanted fancy, I could do fancy...with Olivia's help at least. I smiled at the thought. "Okay."

"Yeah, I changed my mind though."

I laughed. "Well, that was quick."

He laughed as well. "No, I mean, I'll take you somewhere fancy any time you want, but here and now. This is better."

"You're right. I think our morning coffees are one of my favorite things. I fell in love with you here, over coffees and between the words."

"Between the words?"

That wasn't quite what I meant, but I realized it was exactly what I meant. "We had a weird start. There was a lot we didn't say. Like last names and jobs. And on the surface, the things were talked about were commonplace. But somewhere between books and movies, we said a lot. I think I fell in love with you then. Before I knew the rest. Between those simple, basic words, I heard you. I got to know, you. Callum. And that's who I fell in love with."

He nodded. "I understand, though I'm not sure anyone else would. You're right. I fell in love with you here, between coffees and words. And I was right, I don't need someplace fancier to say what I want to say. The words should be said here, where we started."

He reached in his pocket and pulled out a ring. "Alice, will you marry me?"

"Yes," I said without hesitation. He was right, here was exactly where we should make this official.

We kissed again and he put the ring on my finger.

I looked down at it and knew that we had problems ahead of us, but I knew that together we'd figure it out.

We were stronger together than we were apart.

Olivia

Bitty was in her highchair and Mark's father was sitting next to her singing *South Australia*, a song I'd never heard until I met him. It had a quick beat which delighted my daughter.

Everything about Mark's father delighted her.

Mark had remarked that he was surprised by the change in his dad.

They had a little love-fest going on. And his father had been more careful about his health since we started coming around.

I heard Mark come in from the barn.

He greeted me with a kiss. "What's for dinner."

"Soup. Alice's recipe. She said I was safe with it because you can't burn soup."

He laughed. "I'd eat it even if you burned it."

"And that's why I love you," I whispered in his ear as I kissed his cheek.

"Hey Dad, can you watch the soup and the munchkin for a minute?"

"Sure."

He led me out the back door to the porch. There was a cool breeze as we stood and looked out over the farm. "Olivia, I have something to ask you."

Epilogue

Olivia

On the plus side: The only constant is change.
That means we're constantly given the opportunity to start again.

I heard the door to the mudroom open and bang shut. I had Bitty on my hip as I opened the kitchen door.

"Happy birthday," Bitty screamed.

Maybe a stranger wouldn't have recognized her words as that, but no one here was a stranger. Alice was the first one out of her coat and opened her arms. Bitty happily abandoned me.

She babbled excitedly at Alice, Callum, and the kids as everyone shucked off their boots and coats. Callum carried in a present and we all greeted each other with a loud mix of voices.

"The weatherman said over a foot by the lake, more out here," Callum was saying to Mark. They'd become good friends.

Alice and I couldn't have asked for more.

When they bought the old farm down the road from Mark's, they made it clear that Mark should use the acreage as needed for his farm on the condition he helped Alice get started with chickens.

She had ten hens.

Any extra eggs she sent over to Mark for his customers.

Jeremy and Haley helped her name the hens. Which is why one was named Darren, after Jeremy's favorite hockey player. Darren didn't seem to mind that she was named after a hockey player.

The kids told Bitty to name the last hen.

She said Booger. I'd like to say it was because she had a cold, but no matter her intent, Alice had a hen named Boogs.

"Bitty, do you want some cake," Jeremy asked as he swung his sister up. He'd grown inches overnight.

"Someday soon he's going to be taller than both of us," I said to Alice.

I heard someone ring the front doorbell.

It wasn't Alan. He had a new girlfriend and we'd seen less and less of him. We'd invited him to the party, but he said he couldn't make it. He complained about the distance out to the farm. It was about a half hour from Erie, and I knew I'd travel a lot longer than that to be with my daughter.

I sighed. Mark and I both worked at that nonjudgmental thing. Sometimes it was very hard work. I reminded myself that I couldn't control Alan's actions, only my own. And Bitty was surrounded by people who loved her.

The doorbell rang a second time just as I reached for the handle.

"Mom, Dad. I'm glad you made it."

I felt bad that they were front door guests, unlike Alice, Callum, and the kids.

Maybe someday my parents would use the family entrance, but until then, I'd just be happy they'd come.

"Welcome. Let me take your coats."

"Thank you for inviting us," my mother said formally.

My father just nodded.

After Bitty went to town on her cake, Alice pulled me aside. "I need to talk to you. Callum and I aren't saying anything to anyone else yet, but we agreed you could know ... I'm pregnant."

I started to cry.

I really couldn't help myself.

"Me, too," I sniffed.

Callum and Mark heard us and tried to decipher what we were both saying. Finally, one of them made out pregnant and soon all of us were laughing together.

I could see our children, growing up to together on the farm.

A family.

I never wanted the conventional life. I didn't want my mother's life.

I wanted this life.

That was my plus side today and always.

A family.

Alice

That night, after we told Mark, Olivia, Bitty and the rest goodnight, we came home to our house down the road.

The kids had already beaten a path between our house and Olivia's. It wasn't quite as convenient as opening the door in the living room had been, but it worked. They spent as much time on the farm as over here. We all sort of lived between the two houses.

After the kids had gone to bed, Callum sat next to me on the couch, his hand on my stomach and our child.

I never had big dreams.

No, my dreams were built of small things.

Maybe they were dreams of another era.

I dreamed of a man who would love me.

I dreamed of a house filled with children.

I dreamed of a perfect life.

And I'd found that life here, with Callum and our very large—and getting larger—family.

I thought back to that day, two years ago. I couldn't have known then that perfection is overrated.

I didn't understand that the biggest things in life are made up of the smallest ones.

They're built of small moments that grow from other small moments until one day you look back and realize that your life isn't small in the least. Somewhere between the coffees and words, between the heartache and laughter, between the past and the future ... that's where life happens.

And it's certainly not perfect.

Life is imperfect. It's messy.

And that imperfection is the stuff that our dreams are made of.

Life is perfectly imperfect.

And it turns out, so is love.

I kissed Callum and said, "I love you," and thought, on the plus side: a perfectly imperfect life.

Dear Reader,

I so hope you enjoyed Alice and Olivia's stories. When I started the book, I thought I was going to tell just Alice's tale, but as I wrote, I realized how tightly entwined her story was with Olivia's and soon I was telling both stories.

Acceptance.

That is such a hard lesson to learn. Meeting people where they're at and accepting what they're able to give.

Perfection.

That's another hard one.

Learning that we're not perfect and neither is anyone else, and learning to accept them and ourselves...well, that's the point of the story.

I hope you enjoy it as well. Thank you so much for picking up *Between the Words*.

Holly

About the Author:

Award-winning author Holly Jacobs has sold more than three million books worldwide. The first novel in her Everything But... series, *Everything But a Groom*, was named one of 2008's Best Romances by *Booklist*, and her books have been honored with countless other accolades.

Holly has a wide range of interests, from her love for writing to gardening and even basket weaving. She has delivered more than sixty author workshops and keynote speeches across the country. She lives in Erie, Pennsylvania, with her family and her dogs. She frequently sets stories in and around her hometown.

Also by Holly Jacobs

Romance+ Stories
Just One Thing
Same Time Next Summer
Her Second-Chance Family
Between the Words
Words of the Heart Series
Carry Her Heart
These Three Words
Hold Her Heart

Romantic Comedies
I Waxed My Legs for This?
A Day Late and a Bride Short
Bosom Buddies
Cinderella Wore Tennis Shoes

PTA Moms Trilogy
Once Upon a Thanksgiving
Once Upon a Christmas
Once Upon a Valentine's
PTA Mom Collection

Cupid Falls
Christmas in Cupid Falls
A Simple Heart: A Cupid Falls Novella

Short Stories and Novellas
Spoons
The Book
Labor Day
There He Was
13 Weeks
Nothing But Short Story Series:
Nothing But Love
Nothing But Heart
Nothing But Luck
Rather than buy them individually, try:
Short Stories for the Overworked and Under-Read Anthology

Maid in LA Series:
My first mystery series!!
Steamed: A Maid in LA Mystery
Dusted: A Maid in LA Mystery
Spruced Up: A Maid in LA Novella
Swept Up: A Maid in LA Mystery
All four books in one edition
Maid in LA Mysteries bundle
Polished Off: A Maid in LA Mystery

Perry Square Series:
Do You Hear What I Hear?
A Day Late and a Bride Short
Dad Today, Groom Tomorrow
Be My Baby

Once Upon a Princess
Once Upon a Prince
Once Upon a King
Here With Me

Everything But... Series:
Everything But a Groom
Everything But a Bride
Everything But a Wedding
Everything But a Christmas Eve
Everything But a Mother
Everything But a Dog

WLVH Series:
Pickup Lines
Lovehandles
Night Calls
Laugh Lines

Whedon Series:
Unexpected Gifts
A One-of-a-Kind Family
Homecoming Day
A Father's Name

Valley Ridge Series:
You Are Invited... *A Valley Ridge Wedding*
April Showers, *A Valley Ridge Wedding*
A Walk Down the Aisle, *A Valley Ridge Wedding*
A Valley Ridge Christmas

www.ingramcontent.com/pod-product-compliance
Lightning Source LLC
Chambersburg PA
CBHW051434170626
46809CB00006B/2465

* 9 7 8 1 9 4 8 3 1 1 0 0 7 *